Robert Elsmere
Book III

by

Mrs. Humphry Ward

ABOUT THE AUTHOR

Mary Augusta Ward CBE was a British author who lived from June 11, 1851, to March 24, 1920. She wrote under her married name, Mrs. Humphry Ward. Setting up a Settlement in London to help poor people get better schooling was one way she did this. In 1908, she became the first President of the Women's National Anti-Suffrage League. Mary Augusta Arnold was born in Hobart, Tasmania, Australia. She came from a well-known family of writers and educators. Mary was the daughter of Julia Sorell and Tom Arnold, who taught literature. William Thomas Arnold was a writer and journalist, Ethel Arnold worked for women's right to vote, and Julia Huxley started Prior's Field School for Girls in 1902 and married Leonard Huxley. Their sons were Julian and Aldous Huxley. It was important for British intellectual life to have people like the Arnolds and the Huxleys. Author Matthew Arnold was her uncle, and Thomas Arnold, the famous headmaster of Rugby School, was her grandpa. Tom Arnold, Mary's father, was made head of schools in Van Diemen's Land, which is now Tasmania. He started his job on January 15, 1850.

CONTENTS

BOOK III
THE SQUIRE

CHAPTER XIX

The evening of the Murewell Hall dinner-party proved to be a date of some importance in the lives of two or three persons. Rose was not likely to forget it; Langham carried about with him the picture of the great drawing-room, its stately light and shade, and its scattered figures, through many a dismal subsequent hour: and to Robert it was the beginning of a period of practical difficulties such as his fortunate youth had never yet encountered.

His conjecture had hit the mark. The Squire's sentiments toward him, which had been on the whole friendly enough, with the exception of a slight nuance of contempt provoked in Mr. Wendover's mind by all forms of the clerical calling, had been completely transformed in the course of the afternoon before the dinner-party, and transformed by the report of his agent. Henslowe who knew certain sides of the Squire's character by heart, had taken Time by the forelock. For fourteen years before Robert entered the parish he had been king of it. Mr. Preston, Robert's predecessor, had never given him a moment's trouble. The agent had developed a habit of drinking, had favored his friends and spited his enemies, and he allowed certain distant portions of the estate to go finely to ruin, quite undisturbed by any sentimental meddling of the priestly sort. Then the old Rector had been gathered to the majority, and this long-legged busybody had taken his place, a man, according to the agent, as full of communistical notions as an egg is full of meat, and always ready to poke his nose into other people's business. And as all men like mastery, but especially Scotchmen, and as during even the first few months of the new Rector's tenure of office it became tolerably evident to Henslowe that young Elsmere would soon become the ruling force of the neighborhood unless measures were taken to prevent it, the agent, over his nocturnal drams, had taken sharp and cunning counsel with himself concerning the young man.

The state of Mile End had been originally the result of indolence and caprice on his part rather than of any set purpose of neglect. As soon, however, as it was brought to his notice by Elsmere, who did it to begin with, in the friendliest way, it became a point of honor with the agent to let the place go to the devil, nay, to hurry it there. For some time notwithstanding, he avoided an open breach with the Rector. He met Elsmere's remonstrances by a more or less civil show of argument, belied every now and then by the sarcasm of his coarse blue eye, and so far the two men had kept outwardly on terms. Elsmere had reason to know that on one or two occasions of difficulty in the parish Henslowe had tried to do him a mischief. The attempts, however, had not greatly succeeded, and their ill-success had probably excited in Elsmere a confidence of ultimate victory which had tended to keep him cool in the presence of Henslowe's hostility. But Henslowe had been all along merely waiting for the Squire. He had served the owner of the Murewell estate for fourteen years, and if he did not know that owner's peculiarities by this time, might he obtain certain warm corners in the next life to which he was fond of consigning other people! It was not easy to cheat the Squire out of money, but it was quite easy to play upon him ignorance of the details of English land management—ignorance guaranteed by the learned habits of a lifetime—on his complete lack of popular sympathy, and on the contempt felt by the disciple of Bismarck and Mommsen for all forms of altruistic sentiment. The Squire despised priests. He hated philanthropic cants. Above all things be respected his own leisure, and was abnormally, irritably sensitive as to any possible inroads upon it.

All these things Henslowe knew, and all these things be utilized. He saw the Squire within forty-eight hours of his arrival at Murewell. His fancy picture of Robert and his doings was introduced with adroitness, and colored with great skill, and he left the Squire walking up and down his library, chafing alternately at the monstrous fate which had planted this sentimental agitator at his gates, and at the memory of his own misplaced civilities toward the intruder. In the evening those civilities were abundantly avenged, as we have seen.

Robert was much perplexed as to his next step. His heart was very sore. The condition of Mile End—those gaunt-eyed women and wasted children, all the sordid details of their unjust, avoidable suffering weighed upon his nerves perpetually. But he was conscious that this state of feeling was one of tension, perhaps of exaggeration, and though it was impossible he should let the matter alone, he was anxious to do nothing rashly.

However, two days after the dinner-party he met Henslowe on the hill leading up to the Rectory. Robert would have passed the man with a stiffening of his tall figure and the slightest possible salutation. But the agent just returned from a round wherein the bars of various local inns had played a conspicuous part, was in a truculent mood and stopped to speak. He took up the line of insolent condolence with the Rector on the impossibility of carrying his wishes with regard to Mile End into effect. They had been laid before the Squire of course, but the Squire had his own ideas and wasn't just easy to manage.

'Seen him yet, sir?' Henslowe wound up jauntily, every line of his flushed countenance, the full lips under the fair beard, and the light prominent eyes, expressing a triumph he hardly cared to conceal.

'I have seen him, but I have not talked to him on this particular matter,' said the Rector quietly, though the red mounted in his cheek. 'You may, however, be very sure, Mr. Henslowe, that everything I know about Mile End, the Squire shall know before long.'

'Oh, lor' bless me, air!' cried Henslowe with a guffaw, 'it's all one to me. And if the Squire ain't satisfied with the way his work's done now, why he can take you on as a second string you know. You'd show us all, I'll be bound, how to make the money fly.'

Then Robert's temper gave way, and he turned upon the half-drunken brute before him with a few home truths delivered with a rapier-like force which for the moment staggered Henslowe, who turned from red to purple. The Rector, with some of those pitiful memories of the hamlet, of which we had glimpses in his talk with Langham, burning at his heart felt the man no better than a murderer, and as good as told him so. Then, without giving him time to reply, Robert strode off, leaving Henslowe planted in the pathway. But he was hardly up the hill before the agent, having recovered himself by dint of copious expletives, was looking after him with a grim chuckle. He knew his master, and he knew himself, and he thought between them they would about manage to keep that young spark in order.

Robert meanwhile went straight home into his study, and there fell upon ink and paper. What was the good of protracting the matter any longer? Something must and should be done for these people, if not one way, then another.

So he wrote to the Squire, showing the letter to Catherine when it was done, lest there should be anything over-fierce in it. It was the simple record of twelve months' experience told with dignity and strong feeling. Henslowe was barely mentioned in it, and the chief burden of the letter was to implore the Squire to come and inspect certain portions of his property with his own eyes. The Rector would be at his service any day or hour.

Husband and wife went anxiously through the document, softening here, improving there, and then it was sent to the Hall. Robert waited nervously through the day for an answer. In the evening, while he and Catherine were in the footpath after dinner, watching a chilly autumnal moonrise over the stubble of the cornfield, the answer came.

'Hm,' said Robert dubiously as he opened it, holding it up to the moonlight: 'can't be said to be lengthy.'

He and Catherine hurried into the house. Robert read the letter, and handed it to her without a word.

After some curt references to one or two miscellaneous points raised in the latter part of the Rector's letter, the Squire wound up as follows:—

"As for the bulk of your communication, I am at a loss to understand the vehemence of your remarks on the subject of my Mile End property. My agent informed me shortly after my return home that you had been concerning yourself greatly, and, as he conceived, unnecessarily, about the matter. Allow me to assure you that I have full confidence in Mr. Henslowe, who has been in the district for as many years as you have spent months in it, and whose authority on points connected with the business management of my estate naturally carries more weight with me, if you will permit me to say so, than your own.

"*I am, sir, your obedient servant,*

"*ROGER WENDOVER*"

Catherine returned the letter to her husband with a look of dismay. He was standing with his back to the chimney-piece, his hands thrust far into his pockets, his upper lip quivering. In his happy, expansive life this was the sharpest personal rebuff that had ever happened to him. He could not but smart under it.

'Not a word,' he said, tossing his hair bank impetuously, as Catherine stood opposite watching him—'not one single word about the miserable people themselves! What kind of stuff can the man be made of?'

'Does he believe you?' asked Catherine, bewildered.

'If not, one must try and make him,' he said energetically, after a moments pause. 'To-morrow, Catherine, I go down to the Hall and see him.'

She quietly acquiesced, and the following afternoon, first thing after luncheon, she watched him go, her tender inspiring look dwelling with him as he crossed the park, which was lying delicately wrapped in one of the whitest of autumnal mists, the sun just playing through it with pale invading shafts.

The butler looked at him with some doubtfulness. It was never safe to admit visitors for the Squire without orders. But he and Robert had special relations. As the possessor of a bass voice worthy of his girth, Vincent, under Robert's rule, had become the pillar of the choir, and it was not easy for him to refuse the Rector.

So Robert was led in, through the hall, and down the long passage to the curtained door, which he knew so well.

'Mr. Elsmere, Sir!'

There was a sudden, hasty movement. Robert passed a magnificent lacquered screen newly placed round the door, and found himself in the Squire's presence.

The Squire had half risen from his seat in a capacious chair, with a litter of books round it, and confronted his visitor with a look of surprised annoyance. The figure of the Rector, tall, thin, and youthful, stood out against the delicate browns and whites of the book-lined walls. The great room, so impressively bare when Robert and Langham had last seen it, was now full of the signs of a busy man's constant habitation. An odor of smoke pervaded it; the table in the window was piled with books just unpacked, and the half-emptied case from which they had been taken lay on the ground beside the Squire's chair.

'I persuaded Vincent to admit me, Mr. Wendover,' said Robert, advancing hat in hand, while the Squire hastily put down the German professor's pipe he had just been enjoying, and coldly accepted his proffered greeting. 'I should have preferred not to disturb you without an appointment, but after your letter it seemed to me some prompt personal explanation was necessary.'

The Squire stiffly motioned toward a chair, which Robert took, and then slipped back into his own, his wrinkled eyes fixed on the intruder.

Robert, conscious of almost intolerable embarrassment, but maintaining in spite of it an excellent degree of self-control, plunged at once into business. He took the letter he had just received from the Squire as a text, made a good-humored defence of his own proceedings, described his attempt to move Henslowe, and the reluctance of his appeal from the man to the master. The few things he allowed himself to say about Henslowe were in perfect temper, though by no means without an edge.

Then having disposed of the more personal aspects of the matter, he paused, and looked hesitatingly at the face opposite him, more like a bronzed mask at this moment than a human countenance. The Squire, however, gave him no help. He had received his remarks so far in perfect silence, and seeing that there were more to come, he waited for them with the same rigidity of look and attitude.

So, after a moment or two, Robert went on to describe in detail some of those individual cases of hardship and disease at Mile End, during the preceding year, which could be most clearly laid to the sanitary condition of the place. Filth, damp, leaking roofs, foul floors, poisoned water—he traced to each some ghastly human ill, telling his stories with a nervous brevity, a suppressed fire, which would have burnt them into the sense of almost any other listener. Not one of these woes but he and Catherine had tended with sickening pity and labor of body and mind. That side of it he kept rigidly out of sight. But all that he could hurl against the Squire's feeling, as it were, he gathered up, strangely conscious through it all of his own young persistent yearning to right himself with this man, whose mental history, as it lay chronicled in these rooms, had been to him, at a time of intellectual hunger, so stimulating, so enriching.

But passion, and reticence, and bidden sympathy were alike lost upon the Squire. Before he paused Mr. Wendover had already risen restlessly from his chair, and from the rug was glowering down on his, unwelcome visitor.

Good heavens! had he come home to be lectured in his own library by this fanatical slip of a parson? As for his stories, the Squire barely took the trouble to listen to them.

Every popularity-hunting fool, with a passion for putting his hand into other people's pockets, can tell pathetic stories; but it was intolerable that his scholar's privacy should be at the mercy of one of the tribe.

'Mr. Elsmere,' he broke out at last with contemptuous emphasis, 'I imagine it would have been better—infinitely better—to have spared both yourself and me the disagreeables of this interview. However, I am not sorry we should understand each other. I have lived a life which is at least double the length of yours in very tolerable peace and comfort. The world has been good enough for me, and I for it, so far. I have been master in my own estate, and intend to remain so. As for the new-fangled ideas of a landowner's duty, with which your mind seems to be full'—the scornful irritation of the tone was unmistakable—' I have never dabbled in them, nor do I intend to begin now. I am like the rest of my kind; I have no money to chuck away in building schemes, in order that the Rector of the parish may pose as the apostle of the agricultural laborer. That, however, is neither here nor there. What is to the purpose is, that my business affairs are in the hands of a business man, deliberately chosen and approved by me, and that

I have nothing to do with them. Nothing at all!' he repeated with emphasis. 'It may seem to you very shocking. You may reward it as the object in life of the English landowner to inspect the pigstyes and amend the habits of the English laborer. I don't quarrel with the conception, I only ask you not to expect me to live up to it. I am a student first and foremost, and desire to be left to my books. Mr. Henslowe is there on purpose to protect my literary freedom. What he thinks desirable is good enough for me, as I have already informed you. I am sorry for it if his methods do not commend themselves to you. But I have yet to learn that the Rector of the parish has an ex-officio right to interfere between a landlord and his tenants.'

Robert kept his temper with some difficulty. After a pause he said, feeling desperately, however, that the suggestion was not likely to improve matters,—

'If I were to take all the trouble and all the expense off your hands, Mr. Wendover would it be impossible for you to authorize me to make one or two alterations most urgently necessary for the improvement of the Mile End cottages?'

The Squire burst into an angry laugh.

'I have never yet been in the habit, Mr. Elsmere, of doing my repairs by public subscription. You ask a little too much from an old man's powers of adaptation.'

Robert rose from his seat, his hand trembling as it rested on his walking-stick.

'Mr. Wendover,' he said, speaking at last with a flash of answering scorn in his young vibrating voice, 'what I think you cannot understand, is that at any moment a human creature may sicken and die, poisoned by the state of your property, for which you—and nobody else—are ultimately responsible.'

The Squire shrugged his shoulders.

So you say, Mr. Elsmere. If true, every person in such a condition has a remedy in his own hands. I force no one to remain on my property.'

'The people who live there,' exclaimed Robert, 'have neither home nor subsistence if they are driven out. Murewell is full—times bad—most of the people old.'

'And eviction "a sentence of death," I suppose,' interrupted the Squire, studying him with sarcastic eyes. 'Well, I have no belief in a Gladstonian Ireland, still less in a Radical England. Supply and demand, cause and effect, are enough for me. The Mile End cottages are out of repair, Mr. Elsmere, so

Mr. Henslowe tells me, because the site is unsuitable, the type of cottage out of date. People live in them at their peril; I don't pull them down, or rather'—correcting himself with exasperating consistency—'Mr. Henslowe doesn't pull them down, because, like other men, I suppose, he dislikes an outcry. But if the population stays, it stays at its own risk. Now have I made myself plain?'

The two men eyed one another.

'Perfectly plain,' said Robert quietly. 'Allow me to remind you, Mr. Wendover, that there are other matters than eviction capable of provoking an outcry.'

'As you please,' said the other indifferently. 'I have no doubt I shall find myself in the newspapers before long. If so, I dare say I shall manage to put up with it. Society, is fanatics and the creatures they hunt. If I am to be hunted, I shall be in good company.'

Robert stood, hat in hand, tormented with a dozen cross-currents of feeling. He was forcibly struck with the blind and comparatively motiveless pugnacity of the Squire's conduct. There was an extravagance in it which for the first time recalled to him old Meyrick's lucubrations.

'I have done no good, I see, Mr. Wendover,' he said at last, slowly. 'I wish I could have induced you to do an act of justice and mercy. I wish I could have made you think more kindly of myself. I have failed in both. It is useless to keep you any longer. Good morning.'

He bowed. The Squire also bent forward. At that moment Robert caught sight beside his shoulder of an antique, standing on the mantel piece, which was a new addition to the room. It was a head of Medusa, and the frightful stony calm of it struck on Elsmere's ruffled nerves with extraordinary force. It flashed across him that here was an apt symbol of that absorbing and overgrown life of the intellect which blights the heart and chills the senses. And to that spiritual Medusa, the man before him was not the first victim he had known.

Possessed with the fancy, the young man made his way into the hall. Arrived there, he looked round with a kind of passionate regret: 'Shall I ever see this again?' he asked himself. During the past twelve months his pleasure in the great house had been much more than sensuous. Within those walls his mind had grown, had reached to a fuller stature than before, and a man loves, or should love, all that is associated with the maturing of his best self.

He closed the ponderous doors behind him sadly. The magnificent pile, grander than ever in the sunny autumnal mist which unwrapped it, seemed to look after him as he walked away, mutely wondering that he should have allowed anything so trivial as a peasant's grievance to come between him and its perfections.

In the wooded lane outside the Rectory gate he overtook Catherine. He gave her his report, and they walked on together arm-in-arm, a very depressed pair.

'What shall you do next?' she asked him.

'Make out the law of the matter,' he said briefly.

'If you get over the inspector,' said Catherine anxiously, 'I am tolerably certain Henslowe will turn out the people.'

He would not dare, Robert thought. At any rate, the law existed for such cases, and it was his bounden duty to call the inspector's attention.

Catherine' did not see what good could be done thereby, and feared harm. But her wifely chivalry felt that he must get through his first serious practical trouble his own way. She saw that he felt himself distressingly young and inexperienced, and would not for the world have harassed him by over-advice.

So she let him alone, and presently Robert threw the matter from him with a sigh.

'Let it be awhile,' he said with a shake of his long frame. 'I shall get morbid over it if I don't mind. I am a selfish wretch too. I know you have worries of your own, wifie.'

And he took her hand under the trees and kissed it with a boyish tenderness.

'Yes,' said Catherine, sighing, and then paused. 'Robert,' she burst out again, 'I am certain that man made love of a kind to Rose. *He* will never think of it again, but since the night before last she, to my mind, is simply a changed creature.'

'*I* don't see it,' said Robert doubtfully.

Catherine looked at him with a little angel scorn in her gray eyes. That men should make their seeing in such matters the measure of the visible!

'You have been studying the Squire, sir—I have been studying Rose.'

Then she poured out her heart to him, describing the little signs of change and suffering her anxious sense had noted, in spite of Rose's proud effort to keep all the world, but especially Catherine, at arm's length. And at the end her feeling swept her into a denunciation of Langham, which was to Robert like a breath from the past, from those stern hills wherein he met her first. The happiness of their married life had so softened or masked all her ruggedness of character, that there was a certain joy in seeing those strong forces in her which had struck him first reappear.

'Of course I feel myself to blame,' he said when she stopped, 'but how could one foresee, with such an inveterate hermit and recluse? And I owed him—I owe him—so much.'

'I know,' said Catherine, but frowning still. It probably seemed to her that that old debt had been more than effaced.

'You will have to send her to Berlin,' said Elsmere after a pause. 'You must play off her music against this unlucky feeling. If it exists it is your only chance.'

'Yes, she must go to Berlin,' said Catherine slowly.

Then presently she looked up, a flash of exquisite feeling breaking up the delicate resolution of the face.

'I am not sad about that, Robert. Oh, how you have widened my world for me!'

Suddenly that hour in Marrisdale came back to her. They were in the woodpath. She crept inside her husband's arm and put up her face to him, swept away by an overmastering impulse of self-humiliating love.

The next day Robert walked over to the little market town of Churton, saw the discreet and long-established solicitor of the place, and got from him a complete account of the present state of the rural sanitary law. The first step clearly was to move the sanitary inspector; if that failed for any reason, then any *bonâ fide* inhabitant had an appeal to the local sanitary authority, viz. the board of guardians. Robert walked home pondering his information, and totally ignorant that Henslowe, who was always at Churton on market-days, had been in the market-place at the moment when the Rector's tall figure had disappeared within Mr. Dunstan's office-door. That door was unpleasantly known to the agent in connection with some energetic measures for raising money he had been lately under the necessity of employing, and it had a way of attracting his eyes by means of the fascination that often attaches to disagreeable objects.

In the evening Rose was sitting listlessly in the drawing-room. Catherine was not there, so her novel was on her lap and her eyes were staring intently into a world whereof they only had the key. Suddenly there was a ring at the bell. The servant came, and there were several voices and a sound of much shoe-scraping. Then the swing-door leading to the study opened and Elsmere and Catherine came out. Elsmere stopped with an exclamation.

His visitors were two men from Mile End. One was old Milsom, more sallow and palsied than ever. As he stood bent almost double, his old knotted hand resting for support on the table beside him, everything in the little hall seemed to shake with him. The other was Sharland, the handsome father of the twins, whose wife had been fed by Catherine with every imaginable delicacy since Robert's last visit to the hamlet. Even his strong youth had begun to show signs of premature decay. The rolling gypsy eyes were growing sunken, the limbs dragged a little.

They had come to implore the Rector to let Mile End alone. Henslowe had been over there in the afternoon, and had given them all very plainly to understand that if Mr. Elsmere meddled any more they would be all turned out at a week's notice to shift as they could, 'And if you don't find Thurston Common nice lying this weather, with the winter coming on, you'll know who to thank for it,' the agent had flung behind him as he rode off.

Robert turned white. Rose, watching the little scene with listless eyes, saw him towering over the group like an embodiment of wrath and pity.

'If they turn us out, sir,' said old Milsom, wistfully looking up at Elsmere with blear eyes, 'there'll be nothing left but the House for us old 'uns. Why, lor' bless you, sir, it's not so bad but we can make shift.'

'You, Milsom!' cried Robert; 'and you've just all but lost your grandchild! And you know your wife'll never be the same woman since that bout of fever in the spring. And——'

His quick eyes ran over the old man's broken frame with a world of indignant meaning in them.

'Aye, aye, sir,' said Milsom, unmoved. 'But if it isn't fevers, it's summat else. I can make a shilling or two where I be, speshally in the first part of the year, in the basket work, and my wife she goes charing up at Mr. Carter's farm, and Mr. Dodson, him at the further farm, he do give us a bit sometimes. Ef you git us turned away it will be a bad day's work for all on us, sir, you may take my word on it.'

'And my wife so ill' Mr. Elsmere,' said Sharland, 'and all those childer! I can't walk three miles further to my work, Mr. Elsmere, I can't nohow. I haven't got the legs for it. Let un be, Sir. We'll rub along.'

Robert tried to argue the matter.

If they would but stand by him he would fight the matter through, and they should not suffer, if he had to get up a public subscription, or support them out of his own pocket all the winter. A bold front, and Mr. Henslowe must give way. The law was on their side, and every laborer in Surrey would be the better off for their refusal to be housed like pigs and poisoned like vermin.

In vain. There is an inexhaustible store of cautious endurance in the poor against which the keenest reformer constantly throws himself in vain. Elsmere was beaten. The two men got his word, and shuffled off back to their pestilential hovels, a pathetic content beaming on each face.

Catherine and Robert went back into the study. Rose heard her brother-in-law's passionate sigh as the door swung behind them.

'Defeated!' she said to herself with a curious accent. 'Well, everybody must have his turn. Robert has been too successful in his life, I think.—You wretch!' she added, after a minute, laying her bright head down on the book before her.

Next morning his wife found Elsmere after breakfast busily packing a case of books in the study. They were books from the Hall library, which so far had been for months the inseparable companion of his historical work.

Catherine stood and watched him sadly.

'Must You, Robert?'

'I won't be beholden to that man for anything an hour longer than I can help,' he answered her.

When the packing was nearly finished he came up to where she stood in the open window.

'Things won't be as easy for us in the future, darling,' he said to her. 'A rector with both Squire and agent against him is rather heavily handicapped. We must make up our minds to that.'

'I have no great fear,' she said, looking at him proudly.

'Oh, well—nor I—perhaps,' he admitted, after a moment. We can hold our own. 'But I wish—oh, I wish'—and he laid his hand on his wife's shoulder—'I could have made friends with the Squire.'

Catherine looked less responsive.

'As Squire, Robert, or as Mr. Wendover?'

'As both, of course, but specialty as Mr. Wendover.'

'We can do without his friendship,' she said with energy.

Robert gave a great stretch, as though to work off his regrets.

'Ah, but—' he said, half to himself, as his arms dropped, 'if you are just filled with the hunger to *know*, the people who know as much as the Squire become very interesting to you!'

Catherine did not answer. But probably her heart went out once more in protest against a knowledge that was to her but a form of revolt against the awful powers of man's destiny.

'However, here go his books,' said Robert.

Two days later Mrs. Leyburn and Agnes made their appearance, Mrs. Leyburn all in a flutter concerning the event over which, in her own opinion, she had come to preside. In her gentle fluid mind all impressions were short-lived. She had forgotten how she had brought up her own babies, but Mrs. Thornburgh, who had never had any, had filled her full of nursery lore. She sat retailing a host of second-hand hints and instructions to Catherine, who would every now and then lay her hand smiling on her mother's knee, well pleased to see the flush of pleasure on the pretty old face, and ready in her patient filial way, to let herself be experimented on to the utmost, if it did but make the poor, foolish thing happy.

Then came a night where every soul in the quiet Rectory, even hot, smarting Rose, was possessed by one thought though many terrible hours, and one only—the thought of Catherine's safety. It was strange and unexpected, but Catherine, the most normal and healthy of women, had a hard struggle for her own life and her child's, and it was not till the gray autumn morning, after a day and night which left a permanent mark on Robert that he was summoned at last, and with the sense of one emerging from black gulfs of terror, received from his wife's languid hand the tiny fingers of his firstborn.

The days that followed were full of emotion for these two people, who were perhaps always ever-serious, oversensitive. They had no idea of minimizing the great common experiences of life. Both of them were really simple, brought up in old-fashioned simple ways, easily touched, responsive to all that high spiritual education which flows from the familiar incidents of the human story, approached poetically and passionately. As the young husband sat in the quiet of his wife's room, the occasional restless movements of the small brown head against her breast causing the only sound perceptible in the country silence, he felt all the deep familiar currents of human feeling sweeping through him—love, reverence, thanksgiving— and all the walls of the soul, as it were, expanding and enlarging as they passed.

Responsive creature that he was, the experience of these days was hardly happiness. It went too deep; it brought him too poignantly near to all that is most real and therefore most tragic in life.

Catherine's recovery also was slower than might have been expected, considering her constitutional soundness, and for the first week, after that faint moment of joy when her child was laid upon her arm and she saw her husband's quivering face above her, there was a kind of depression hovering over her. Robert felt it, and felt too that all his devotion could not soothe it away. At last she said to him one evening, in the encroaching September twilight, speaking with a sudden hurrying vehemence, wholly unlike herself, as though a barrier of reserve had given way,—

'Robert, I cannot put it out of my head. I cannot forget it, *the pain of the world!'*

He shut the book he was reading, her hand in his, and bent over her with questioning eyes.

'It seems' she went on with that difficulty which a strong nature always feels in self-revelation, 'to take the joy even out of our love—and the child. I feel ashamed almost that mere physical pain should have laid such hold on me—and yet I can't get away from it. It's not for myself,' and she smiled faintly at him. 'Comparatively I had so little to bear! But I know now for the first time what physical pain may mean—and I never knew before! I lie thinking, Robert, about all creatures in pain—workmen crushed by machinery, or soldiers—or poor things in hospitals—above all of women! Oh, when I get well, how I will take care of the women here! What women must suffer even here in out-of-the-way cottages—no doctor, no kind nursing, all blind agony and struggle! And women in London in dens like those Mr. Newcome got into, degraded, forsaken, ill-treated, the thought of the child only an extra horror and burden! And the pain all the time so merciless, so cruel—no escape! Oh, to give all one is, or ever can be, to comforting! And yet the great sea of it one can never touch! It is a nightmare—I am weak still, I suppose; I don't know myself; but I can see nothing but jarred, tortured creatures everywhere. All my own joys and comforts seem to lift me selfishly above the common lot.'

She stopped, her large gray-blue eyes dim with tears, trying once more for that habitual self-restraint which physical weakness had shaken.

'You *are* weak,' he said, caressing her, 'and that destroys for a time the normal balance of things. It is true, darling, but we are not meant to see it always so clearly. God knows we could not bear it if we did.'

And to think,' she said, shuddering a little, 'that there are men and women who in the face of it can still refuse Christ and the Cross, can still say this life is all! How can they live—how dare they live?'

Then he saw that not only man's pain but man's defiance, had been haunting her, and he guessed what persons and memories had been flitting through her mind. But he dared not talk lest she should exhaust herself. Presently, seeing a volume of Augustine's 'Confessions', her favorite book, lying beside her, he took it up, turning over the pages, and weaving passages together as they caught his eye.

'Speak to me, for Thy compassion's sake, O Lord my God, and tell me what art Thou to me! Say unto my soul, "I am thy salvation." Speak it that I may hear. Behold the ears of my heart, O Lord; open them and say into my soul, "I am thy salvation!" I will follow after this voice of Thine, I will lay hold on Thee. The temple of my soul, wherein Thou shouldest enter, is narrow, do Thou enlarge it. It falleth into ruins—do Thou rebuild it!... Woe to that bold soul which hopeth, if it do but let Thee go, to find something better than Thee! It turneth hither and thither, on this side and on that, and all things are hard and bitter unto it. For Thou only art rest!... Whithersoever the soul of man turneth it findeth sorrow, except only in Thee. Fix there, then, thy resting-place, mm soul! Lay up in Him whatever thou hast received from Him. Commend to the keeping of the Truth whatever the Truth hath given thee, and thou shalt lose nothing. And thy dead things shall revive and thy weak things shall be made whole!'

She listened, appropriating and clinging to every word, till the nervous clasp of the long delicate fingers relaxed, her head dropped a little, gently, against the head of the child, and tired with much feeling she slept.

Robert slipped away and strolled out into the garden in the fast-gathering darkness. His mind was full of that intense spiritual life of Catherine's which in its wonderful self-contentedness and strength was always a marvel, sometimes a reproach to him. Beside her, he seemed to himself a light creature, drawn hither and thither by this interest and by that, tangled in the fleeting shows of things—the toy and plaything of circumstance. He thought ruefully and humbly, as he wondered on through the dusk, of his own lack of inwardness: 'Everything divides me from Thee!' he could have cried in St. Augustine's manner. 'Books, and friends, and work—all seem to hide Thee from me. Why am I so passionate for this and that, for all these sections and fragments of Thee? Oh, for the One, the All! Fix, there thy resting-place, my soul!'

And presently, after this cry of self-reproach, he turned to muse on that intuition of the world's pain which had been troubling Catherine, shrinking from it even more than she had shrunk from it, in proportion as his nature was more imaginative than hers. And Christ the only clew, the only remedy—no other anywhere in this vast Universe, where all men are under sentences of death, where the whole creation groaneth and travaileth in pain together until now!

And yet what countless generations of men had borne their pain, knowing nothing of the one Healer. He thought of Buddhist patience and Buddhist charity; of the long centuries during which Chaldean or Persian or Egyptian lived, suffered, and died, trusting the gods they knew. And how many other generations, nominally children of the Great Hope, had used it as a mere instrument of passion or of hate, cursing in the name of love, destroying in the name of pity! For how much of the world's pain was not Christianity itself responsible? His thoughts recurred with a kind of anguished perplexity to some of the problems stirred in him of late by his historical reading. The strifes and feuds and violences of the early Church returned to weigh upon him—the hair-splitting superstition, the selfish passion for power. He recalled Gibbon's lamentation over the age of the Antonines, and Mommsen's grave doubt whether, taken as a whole, the area once covered by the Roman Empire can be said to be substantially happier now than in the days of Severus.

O corruptio optimi! That men should have been so little affected by that shining ideal of the New Jerusalem, 'descended out of Heaven from God,' into their very midst—that the print of the 'blessed feet' along the world's highway should have been so often buried in the sands of cruelty and fraud!

The September wind blew about him as he strolled through the darkening common, set thick with great bushes of sombre juniper among the yellowing fern, which stretched away on the left-hand side of the road leading to the Hall. He stood and watched the masses of restless discordant cloud which the sunset had left behind it, thinking the while of Mr. Grey, of his assertions and his denials. Certain phrases of his which Robert had heard drop from him on one or two rare occasions during the later stages of his Oxford life ran through his head.

'*The fairy-tale of Christianity*'—'*The origins of Christian Mythology.*' He could recall, as the words rose in his memory, the simplicity of the rugged face, and the melancholy mingled with fire which had always marked the great tutor's sayings about religion.

'*Fairy Tale!*' Could any reasonable man watch a life like Catherine's and believe that nothing but a delusion lay at the heart of it? And as he asked the question, he seemed to hear Mr. Grey's answer: 'All religions are true and all are false. In them all, more or less visibly, man grasps at the one thing needful—self forsaken, God laid hold of. The spirit in them all is the same, answers eternally to reality; it is but the letter, the fashion, the imagery, that are relative and changing.'

He turned and walked homeward, struggling with a host of tempestuous ideas as swift and varying as the autumn clouds hurrying overhead. And then, through a break in a line of trees, he caught sight of the tower and chancel window of the little church. In an instant he had a vision of early summer mornings—dewy, perfumed, silent, save for the birds and all the soft stir of rural birth and growth, of a chancel fragrant with many flowers, of a distant church with scattered figures, of the kneeling form of his wife close beside him, himself bending over her, the sacrament of the Lord's death in his hand. The emotion, the intensity, the absolute self-surrender of innumerable such moments in the past—moments of a common faith, a common self-abasement—came flooding back upon him. With a movement of joy and penitence he threw himself at the feet of Catherine's Master and his own: *'Fix there thy resting-place, my soul!'*

CHAPTER XX

Catherine's later convalescence dwelt in her mind in after years as a time of peculiar softness and peace. Her baby-girl throve; Robert had driven the Squire and Henslowe out of his mind, and was all eagerness as to certain negotiations with a famous naturalist for a lecture at the village club. At Mile End, as though to put the Rector in the wrong, serious illness had for the time disappeared; and Mrs. Leyburn's mild chatter, as she gently poked about the house and garden, went out in Catherine's pony-carriage, inspected Catherine's stores, and hovered over Catherine's babe, had a constantly cheering effect on the still languid mother. Like all theorists, especially those at secondhand, Mrs. Leyburn's maxims had been very much routed by the event. The babe had ailments she did not understand, or it developed likes and dislikes she had forgotten existed in babies, and Mrs. Leyburn was nonplussed. She would sit with it on her lap, anxiously studying its peculiarities. She was sure it squinted, that its back was weaker than other babies, that it cried more than hers had ever done. She loved to be plaintive; it would have seemed to her unladylike to be too cheerful, even over a first grandchild.

Agnes meanwhile made herself practically useful, as was her way, and she did almost more than anybody to beguile Catherine's recovery by her hours of Long Whindale chat. She had no passionate feeling about the place and the people as Catherine had, but she was easily content, and she had a good wholesome feminine curiosity as to the courtings and weddings and buryings of the human beings about her. So she would sit and chat, working the while with the quickest, neatest of fingers, till Catherine knew as much about Jenny Tyson's Whinborough lover, and Farmer Tredall's troubles with his son, and the way in which that odious woman Molly Redgold bullied her little consumptive husband, as Agnes knew, which was saying a good deal.

About themselves Agnes was frankness itself.

'Since you went,' she would say with a shrug, 'I keep the coach steady, perhaps, but Rose drives, and we shall have to go where she takes us. By the way, Cathie, what have you been doing to her here? She is not a bit like herself. I don't generally mind being snubbed. It amuses her and doesn't hurt me; and, of course, I know I am meant to be her foil. But really, sometimes she is too bad even for me.'

Catherine sighed, but held her peace. Like all strong persons, she kept things very much to herself. It only made vexation more real to talk about them. But she and Agnes discussed the winter and Berlin.

'You had better let her go,' said Agnes, significantly; 'she will go anyhow.'

A few days afterward Catherine, opening the drawing-room door unexpectedly, came upon Rose sitting idly at the piano, her hands resting on the keys, and her great gray eyes straining out of her white face with an expression which sent the sister's heart into her shoes.

'How you steal about, Catherine!' cried the player, getting up and shutting the piano. 'I declare you are just like Millais's Gray Lady in that ghostly gown.'

Catherine came swiftly across the floor. She had just left her child, and the sweet dignity of motherhood was in her step, her look. She came and threw her arms round the girl.

'Rose dear, I have settled it all with mamma. The money can be managed, and you shall go to Berlin for the winter when you like.'

She drew herself back a little, still with her arms round Rose's waist, and looked at her smiling, to see how she took it.

Rose had a strange movement of irritation. She drew herself out of Catherine's grasp.

'I don't know that I had settled on Berlin,' she said coldly, 'Very possibly Leipsic would be better.'

Catherine's face fell.

'Whichever you like, dear. I have been thinking about it ever since that day you spoke of it—you remember—and now I have talked it over with mamma. If she can't manage, all the expense we will help. Oh Rose,' and she came nearer again, timidly, her eyes melting, 'I know we haven't understood each other. I have been ignorant, I think, and narrow. But I meant it for the best, dear—I did—'

Her voice failed her, but in her look there seemed to be written the history of all the prayers and yearnings of her youth over the pretty wayward child who had been her joy and torment. Rose could not but meet that look—its nobleness, its humble surrender.

Suddenly two large tears rolled down her cheeks. She dashed them away impatiently.

'I am not a bit well,' she said, as though in irritable excuse both to herself and Catherine. 'I believe I have had a headache for a fortnight.'

And then she put her arms down on a table near and hid her face upon them. She was one bundle of jarring nerves; sore, poor passionate child, that she was betraying herself; sorer still that, as she told herself, Catherine was sending her to Berlin as a consolation. When girls have love-troubles the first thing their elders do is to look for a diversion. She felt sick and humiliated. Catherine had been talking her over with the family, she supposed.

Meanwhile Catherine stood by her tenderly, stroking her hair and saying soothing things.

'I am sure you will be happy at Berlin, Rose. And you mustn't leave me out of your life, dear, though I am so stupid and unmusical. You must write to me about all you do. We must be in a new time. Oh, I feel so guilty sometimes,' she went on, falling into a low intensity of voice that startled Rose, and made her look hurriedly up. 'I fought against your music, I suppose, because I thought it was devouring you—leaving no room for— for religion—for God. I was jealous of it for Christ's sake. And all the time I was blundering! Oh, Rose,' and she sank on her knees beside the chair, resting her head against the girl's shoulder, 'papa charged me to make you love God, and I torture myself with thinking that, instead, it has been my doing, my foolish, clumsy doing, that you have come to think religion dull and hard. Oh, my darling, if I could make amends—if I could got you not to love your art less but to love it in God! Christ is the first reality; all things else are real and lovely in Him! Oh, I have been frightening you away from Him! I ought to have drawn you near. I have been so—so silent, so shut up, I have never tried to make you feel what it was kept *me* at His feet! Oh, Rose darling, you think the world real, and pleasure and enjoyment real. But if I could have made you see and know the things I have seen up in the mountains—among the poor, the dying—you would have *felt* Him saving, redeeming, interceding, as I did. Oh, then you *must*, you *would* have known that Christ only is real, that our joys can only truly exist in Him. I should have been more open—more faithful—more humble.'

She paused with a long quivering sigh. Rose suddenly lifted herself, and they fell into each others' arms.

Rose, shaken and excited, thought, of course, of that night at Burwood, when she had won leave to go to Manchester. This scene was the sequel to that—the next stage in one and the same process. Her feeling was much the same as that of the naturalist who comes close to any of the hidden operations of life. She had come near to Catherine's spirit in the growing. Beside that sweet expansion, how poor and feverish and earth-stained the poor child felt herself!

But there were many currents in Rose—many things striving for the mastery. She kissed Catherine once or twice, then she drew herself back suddenly, looking into the other's face. A great wave of feeling rushed up and broke.

'Catherine, could you ever have married a man that did not believe in Christ?'

She flung the question out—a kind of morbid curiosity, a wild wish to find an outlet of some sort for things pent up in her, driving her on.

Catherine started. But she met Rose's half-frowning eyes steadily.

'Never, Rose! To me it would not be marriage.' The child's face lost its softness. She drew one hand away.

'What have we to do with it?' She cried. 'Each one for himself.'

'But marriage makes two one,' said Catherine, pale, but with a firm clearness. 'And if husband and wife are only one in body and estate, not one in soul, why who that believes in the soul would accept such a bond, endure such a miserable second best?'

She rose. But though her voice had recovered all its energy, her attitude, her look was still tenderness, still yearning itself.

'Religion does not fill up the soul,' said Rose slowly. Then she added carelessly, a passionate red flying into her cheek, against her will, 'However, I cannot imagine any question that interests me personally less. I was curious what you would say.'

And she too got up, drawing her hand lightly along the keyboard of the piano. Her pose had a kind of defiance in it; her knit brows forbade Catherine to ask questions. Catherine stood irresolute. Should she throw herself on her sister, imploring her to speak, opening her own heart on the subject of this wild, unhappy fancy for a man who would never think again of the child he had played with?

But the North-country dread of words, of speech that only defines and magnifies, prevailed. Let there be no words, but let her love and watch.

So, after a moment's pause, she began in a different tone upon the inquiries she had been making, the arrangements that would be wanted for this musical winter. Rose was almost listless at first. A stranger would have thought she was being persuaded into something against her will. But she could not keep it up. The natural instinct reasserted itself, and she was soon planning and deciding as sharply, and with as much young omniscience, as usual.

By the evening it was settled. Mrs. Leyburn, much bewildered, asked Catherine doubtfully, the last thing at night, whether she wanted Rose to be a professional. Catherine exclaimed.

'But, my dear,' said the widow, staring pensively into her bedroom fire, 'what's she to do with all this music?' Then after a second she added half severely: 'I don't believe her father would have liked it; I don't, indeed, Catherine!'

Poor Catherine smiled and sighed in the background, but made no reply.

'However, she never looks so pretty as when she's playing the violin; never!' said Mrs. Leyburn presently in the distance, with a long breath of satisfaction. 'She's got such a lovely hand and arm, Catherine! They're prettier than mine, and even your father used to notice mine.'

'*Even.*' The word had a little sound of bitterness. In spite of all his love, had the gentle puzzle-headed woman found her unearthly husband often very hard to live with?

Rose meanwhile was sitting up in bed, with her hands round her knees, dreaming. So she had got her heart's desire! There did not seem to be much joy in the getting, but that was the way of things, one was told. She knew she should hate the Germans—great, bouncing, over-fed, sentimental creatures!

Then her thoughts ran into the future. After six months—yes, by April— she would be home, and Agnes and her mother could meet her in London.

London. Ah, it was London she was thinking of all the time, not Berlin! She could not stay in the present; or rather the Rose of the present went straining to the Rose of the future, asking to be righted, to be avenged.

'I will learn—I will learn fast, many things besides music!' she said to herself feverishly. 'By April I shall be *much* cleverer. Oh, *then* I won't be a fool so easily. We shall be sure to meet, of course. But he shall find out that it was only a *child*, only a silly, softhearted baby he played with down here. I shan't care for him in the least, of course not, not after six months. I don't *mean* to. And I will make him know it—oh, I will, though he is so wise, and so much older, and mounts on such stilts when he pleases!'

So once more Rose flung her defiance at fate. But when Catherine came along the passage an hour later she heard low sounds from Rose's room, which ceased abruptly as her step drew near. The elder sister paused; her eyes filled with tears; her hand closed indignantly. Then she came closer, all but went in, thought better of it, and moved away. If there is any truth in brain waves, Langham should have slept restlessly that night.

Ten days later an escort had been found, all preparations had been made, and Rose was gone.

Mrs. Leyburn and Agnes lingered a while, and then they too departed under an engagement to come back after Christmas for a long stay, that Mrs. Leyburn might cheat the Northern spring a little.

So husband and wife were alone again. How they relished their solitude! Catherine took up many threads of work which her months of comparative weakness had forced her to let drop. She taught vigorously in the school; in the afternoons, so far as her child would let her, she carried her tender presence and her practical knowledge of nursing to the sick and feeble; and on two evenings in the week she and Robert threw open a little room there was on the ground-floor between the study and the dining-room to the women and girls of the village, as a sort of drawing-room. Hard-worked mothers would come, who had put their fretful babes to sleep, and given their lords to eat, and had just energy left, while the eldest daughter watched, and the men were at the club or the 'Blue Boar,' to put on a clean apron and climb the short hill to the rectory. Once there, there was nothing to think of for an hour but the bright room, Catherine's kind face, the Rector's jokes, and the illustrated papers or the photographs that were spread out for them to look at if they would. The girls learned to come, because Catherine could teach them a simple dressmaking, and was clever in catching stray persons to set them singing; and because Mr. Elsmere read exciting stories, and because nothing any one of them ever told Mrs. Elsmere was forgotten by her, or failed to interest her. Any of her social equals of the neighborhood would have hardly recognized the reserved and stately Catherine on these occasions. Here she felt herself at home, at ease. She would never, indeed, have Robert's pliancy, his quick divination, and for some time after her transplanting the North-country woman had found it very difficult to suit herself to a new shade of local character. But she was learning from Robert every day; she watched him among the poor, recognizing all his gifts with a humble intensity of admiring love, which said little but treasured everything, and for herself her inward happiness and peace shone through her quiet ways, making her the mother and the friend of all about her.

As for Robert, he, of course, was living at high pressure all round. Outside his sermons and his school, his Natural History Club had perhaps most of his heart, and the passion for science, little continuous work as he was able to give it, grew on him more and more. He kept up as best he could, working with one hand, so to speak, when he could not spare two, and in his long rambles over moor and hill, gathering in with his quick eye a harvest of local fact wherewith to feed their knowledge and his own.

The mornings he always spent at work among his books, the afternoons in endless tramps over the parish, sometimes alone, sometimes with Catherine; and in the evenings, if Catherine was 'at home' twice a week to womankind, he had his nights when his study became the haunt and prey of half the boys in the place, who were free of everything, as soon as he had taught them to respect his books, and not to taste his medicines; other nights when he was lecturing or story-telling, in the club or in some outlying hamlet; or others again, when with Catherine beside him he would sit trying to think some of that religious passion which burned in both their hearts, into clear words or striking illustrations for his sermons.

Then his choir was much upon his mind. He knew nothing about music, nor did Catherine; their efforts made Rose laugh irreverently when she got their letters at Berlin. But Robert believed in a choir chiefly as an excellent social and centralizing instrument. There had been none in Mr. Preston's day. He was determined to have one, and a good one, and by sheer energy he succeeded, delighting in his boyish way over the opposition some of his novelties excited among the older and more stiff-backed inhabitants.

'Let them talk,' he would say brightly to Catherine. 'They will come round; and talk is good. Anything to make them think, to stir the pool!'

Of course that old problem of the agricultural laborer weighed upon him—his grievances, his wants. He went about pondering the English land system, more than half inclined one day to sink part of his capital in a peasant-proprietor experiment, and engulfed the next in all the moral and economical objections to the French system. Land for allotments, at any rate, he had set his heart on. But in this direction, as in many others, the way was barred. All the land in the parish was the Squire's, and not an inch of the Squire's land would Henslowe let young Elsmere have anything to do with if he knew it. He would neither repair, nor enlarge the Workmen's Institute; and he had a way of forgetting the Squire's customary subscriptions to parochial objects, always paid through him, which gave him much food for chuckling whenever he passed Elsmere in the country lanes. The man's coarse insolence and mean hatred made themselves felt at every turn, besmirching and embittering.

Still it was very true that neither Henslowe nor the Squire could do Robert much harm. His hold on the parish was visibly strengthening; his sermons were not only filling the church with his own parishioners, but attracting hearers from the districts round Murewell, so that even on these winter Sundays there was almost always a sprinkling of strange faces among the congregation; and his position in the county and diocese was becoming every month more honorable and important. The gentry about showed them much kindness, and would have shown them much hospitality if they had been allowed. But though Robert had nothing of the ascetic about him, and liked the society of his equals as much as most good-tempered and vivacious people do, he and Catherine decided that for the present they had no time to spare for visits and county society. Still, of course, there were many occasions on which the routine of their life brought them across their neighbors, and it began to be pretty widely recognized that Elsmere was a young fellow of unusual promise and intelligence, that his wife too was remarkable, and that between them they were likely to raise the standard of clerical effort considerably in their part of Surrey.

All the factors of this life—his work, his influence, his recovered health, the lavish beauty of the country, Elsmere enjoyed with all his heart. But at the root of all there lay what gave value and savor to everything else—that exquisite home-life of theirs, that tender, triple bond of husband, wife, and child.

Catherine coming home tired from teaching or visiting, would find her step quickening as she reached the gate of the rectory, and the sense of delicious possession waking up in her, which is one of the first fruits of motherhood. There, at the window, between the lamplight behind and the winter dusk outside, would be the child in its nurse's arms, little wondering, motiveless smiles passing over the tiny puckered face that was so oddly like Robert already. And afterward, in the fire-lit nursery, with the bath in front of the high fender, and all the necessaries of baby life beside it, she would go through those functions which mothers love and linger over, let the kicking, dimpled creature principally concerned protest as it may against the over-refinements of civilization. Then, when the little restless voice was stilled, and the cradle left silent in the darkened room, there would come the short watching for Robert, his voice, his kiss, their simple meal together, a moment of rest, of laughter and chat, before some fresh effort claimed them. Every now and then—white-letter days—there would drop on them a long evening together. Then out would come one of the few books— Dante or Virgil or Milton—which had entered into the fibre of Catherine's strong nature. The two heads would draw close over them, or Robert would take some thought of hers as a text, and spout away from the hearthrug, watching all the while for her smile, her look of assent. Sometimes, late at night, when there was a sermon on his mind, he would dive into his pocket for his Greek Testament and make her read, partly for the sake of teaching her—for she knew some Greek and longed to know more—but mostly that he might get from her some of that garnered wealth of spiritual experience which he adored in her. They would go from verse to verse, from thought to thought, till suddenly perhaps the tide of feeling would rise, and while the windswept round the house, and the owls hooted in the elms, they would sit hand in hand, lost in love and fait—Christ near them—Eternity, warm with God, enwrapping them.

So much for the man of action, the husband, the philanthropist. In reality, great as was the moral energy of this period of Elsmere's life, the dominant distinguishing note of it was not moral but intellectual.

In matters of conduct he was but developing habits and tendencies already strongly present in him; in matters of his thinking, with every month of this winter he was becoming conscious of fresh forces, fresh hunger, fresh horizons.

'*One half of your day be the king of your world,*' Mr. Grey had said to him; '*the other half be the slave of something which will take you out of your world,* into the general life, the life of thought, of man as a whole, of the universe.'

The counsel, as we have seen, had struck root and flowered into action. So many men of Elsmere's type give themselves up once and for all as they become mature to the life of doing and feeling, practically excluding the life of thought. It was Henry Grey's influence in all probability, perhaps, too, the training of an earlier Langham, that saved for Elsmere the life of thought.

The form taken by this training of his own mind he had been thus encouraged not to abandon, was, as we know, the study of history. He had well mapped out before him that book on the origins of France which he had described to Langham. It was to take him years, of course, and meanwhile, in his first enthusiasm, he was like a child, revelling in the treasure of work that lay before him. As he had told Langham, he had just got below the surface of a great subject and was beginning to dig into the roots of it. Hitherto he had been under the guidance of men of his own day, of the nineteenth century historian, who refashions the past on the lines of his own mind, who gives it rationality, coherence, and, as it were, modernness, so that the main impression he produces on us, so long as we look at that past through him only, is on the whole an impression of continuity of *resemblance*.

Whereas, on the contrary, the first impression left on a man by the attempt to plunge into the materials of history for himself is almost always an extraordinarily sharp impression of *difference*, of *contrast*. Ultimately, of course, he sees that those men and women whose letters and biographies, whose creeds and general conceptions he is investigating, are in truth his ancestors, bone of his bone, flesh of his flesh. But at first the student who goes back, say, in the history of Europe, behind the Renaissance or behind the Crusades into the actual deposits of the past, is often struck with a kind of *vertige*. The men and women whom he has dragged forth into the light of his own mind are to him like some strange puppet-show. They are called by names he knows—kings, bishops, judges, poets, priests, men of letters—but what a gulf between him and them! What motives, what beliefs, what embryonic processes of thought and morals, what bizarre combinations of ignorance and knowledge, of the highest sanctity with the lowest credulity or falsehood; what extraordinary prepossessions, born with a man and tainting his whole ways of seeing and thinking from childhood to the grave! Amid all the intellectual dislocation of the spectacle, indeed, he perceives certain Greeks and certain Latins who represent a forward strain, who belong as it seems to a world of their own, a world ahead of them. To them he stretches out his hand: '*You*,' he says to them, 'though your priests spoke to you not of Christ, but of Zeus and Artemis, *you* are really my kindred!' But intellectually they stand alone. Around them, after them, for long ages the world 'spake as a child, felt as a child, understood as a child.'

Then he sees what it is makes the difference, digs the gulf. '*Science*,' the mind cries, '*ordered knowledge*.' And so for the first time the modern recognizes what the accumulations of his forefathers have done for him. He takes the torch which man has been so long and patiently fashioning to his hand, and turns it on the past, and at every step the sight grows stranger, and yet more moving, more pathetic. The darkness into which he penetrates does but make him grasp his own guiding light the more closely. And yet, bit by bit, it has been prepared for him by these groping, half-conscious generations, and the scrutiny which began in repulsion and laughter ends in a marvelling gratitude.

But the repulsion and the laughter come first, and during this winter of work Elsmere felt them both very strongly. He would sit in the morning buried among the records of decaying Rome and emerging France, surrounded by Chronicles, by Church Councils, by lives of the Saints, by primitive systems of law, pushing his imaginative, impetuous way through them. Sometimes Catherine would be there, and he would pour out on her something of what was in his own mind.

One day he was deep in the life of a certain saint. The saint had been bishop of a diocese in Southern France. His biographer was his successor in the see, a man of high political importance in the Burgundian state, renowned besides for sanctity and learning. Only some twenty years separated the biography, at the latest, from the death of its subject. It contained some curious material for social history, and Robert was reading it with avidity.

But it was, of course, a tissue of marvels. The young bishop had practised every virtue known to the time, and wrought every conceivable miracle, and the miracles were better told than usual, with more ingenuity, more imagination. Perhaps on that account they struck the reader's sense more sharply.

'And the saint said to the sorcerers and to the practisers of unholy arts, that they should do those evil things no more, for he had bound the spirits of whom they were wont to inquire, and they would get no further answers to their incantations. Then those stiff-necked sons of the Devil fell upon the man of God, scourged him sore, and threatened him with death, if he would not instantly loose those spirits he had bound. And seeing he could prevail nothing, and being moreover, admonished by God so to do, he permitted them to work their own damnation. For he called for a parchment and wrote upon it, "*Ambrose unto Satan — Enter!*" Then was the spell loosed, the spirits returned, the sorcerers inquired as they were accustomed, and received answers. But in a short space of time every one of them perished miserably and was delivered unto his natural lord Satanas, whereunto he belonged.'

Robert made a hasty exclamation, and turning to Catherine, who was working beside him, read the passage to her, with a few words as to the book and its author.

Catherine's work dropped a moment on to her knee.

'What extraordinary superstition!' she said, startled. 'A bishop, Robert, and an educated man?'

Robert nodded.

'But it is the whole habit of mind,' he said half to himself, staring into the fire, 'that is so astounding. No one escapes it. The whole age really is non-sane.'

'I suppose the devout Catholic would believe that?'

'I am not sure,' said Robert dreamily, and remained sunk in thought for long after, while Catherine worked, and pondered a Christmas entertainment for her girls.

Perhaps it was his scientific work, fragmentary as it was that was really quickening and sharpening these historical impressions of his. Evolution — once a mere germ in the mind — was beginning to press, to encroach, to intermeddle with the mind's other furniture.

And the comparative instinct — that tool, *par excellence*, of modern science was at last fully awake, was growing fast, taking hold, now here, now there.

'It is tolerably clear to me,' he said to himself suddenly one winter afternoon, as he was trudging home alone from Mile End, 'that some day or other I must set to work to bring a little order into one's notions of the Old Testament. At present they are just a chaos!'

He walked on awhile, struggling with the rainstorm which had overtaken him, till again the mind's quick life took voice.

'But what matter? God in the beginning—God in the prophets—in Israel's best life—God in Christ! How are any theories about the Pentateuch to touch that?'

And into the clear eyes, the young face aglow with wind and rain, there leapt a light, a softness indescribable.

But the vivider and the keener grew this new mental life of Elsmere's, the more constant became his sense of soreness as to that foolish and motiveless quarrel which divided him from the Squire. Naturally he was for ever being harassed and pulled up in his work by the mere loss of the Murewell library. To have such a collection so close, and to be cut off from it, was a state of things no student could help feeling severely. But it was much more than that: it was the man he hankered after; the man who was a master where he was a beginner; the man who had given his life to learning, and was carrying all his vast accumulations sombrely to the grave, unused, untransmitted.

'He might have given me his knowledge,' thought Elsmere sadly, 'and I—I—would have been a son to him. Why is life so perverse?'

Meanwhile he was as much cut off from the great house and its master as though both had been surrounded by the thorn hedge of fairy tale. The Hall had its visitors during these winter months, but the Elsmeres saw nothing of them. Robert gulped down a natural sigh when one Saturday evening, as he passed the Hall gates, he saw driving through them the chief of English science side by side with the most accomplished of English critics.

"'There are good times in the world and I ain't in 'em!'" he said to himself with a laugh and a shrug as he turned up the lane to the rectory, and then, boylike, was ashamed of himself, and greeted Catherine, with all the tenderer greeting.

Only on two occasions during three months could he be sure of having seen the Squire. Both were in the twilight, when, as the neighborhood declared, Mr. Wendover always walked, and both made a sharp impression on the Rector's nerves. In the heart of one of the loneliest commons of the parish Robert, swinging along one November evening through the scattered furze bushes growing ghostly in the darkness, was suddenly conscious of a cloaked figure with slouching shoulders and head bent forward coming toward him. It passed without recognition of any kind, and for an instant Robert caught the long, sharpened features and haughty eyes of the Squire.

At another time Robert was walking, far from home, along a bit of level road. The pools in the ruts were just filmed with frost, and gleamed under the sunset; the winter dusk was clear and chill. A horseman turned into the road from a side lane. It was the Squire again, alone. The sharp sound of the approaching hoofs stirred Robert's pulse, and as they passed each other the Rector raised his hat. He thought his greeting was acknowledged, but could not be quite sure. From the shelter of a group of trees he stood a moment and looked after the retreating figure. It and the horse showed dark against a wide sky barred by stormy reds and purples. The wind whistled through the withered oaks; the long road with its lines of glimmering pools seemed to stretch endlessly into the sunset; and with every minute the night strode on. Age and loneliness could have found no fitter setting. A shiver ran through Elsmere as he stepped forward.

Undoubtedly the quarrel, helped by his work, and the perpetual presence of that beautiful house commanding the whole country round it from its plateau above the river, kept Elsmere specially in mind of the Squire. As before their first meeting, and in spite of it, he became more and more imaginatively preoccupied with him. One of the signs of it was a strong desire to read the Squire's two famous books: one, 'The Idols of the Market Place,' an attack on English beliefs; the other, 'Essays on English Culture,' an attack on English ideals of education. He had never come across them as it happened, and perhaps Newcome's denunciation had some effect in inducing him for a time to refrain from reading them. But in December he ordered them and waited their coming with impatience. He said nothing of the order to Catherine; somehow there were by now two or three portions of his work, two or three branches of his thought, which had fallen out of their common discussion. After all she was not literary and with all their oneness of soul there could not be an *identity* of interests or pursuits.

The books arrived in the morning. (Oh, how dismally well, with what a tightening of the heart, did Robert always remember that day in after years!) He was much too busy to look at them, and went off to a meeting. In the evening, coming home late from his night-school, he found Catherine tired, sent her to bed, and went himself into his study to put together some notes for a cottage lecture he was to give the following day. The packet of books, unopened, lay on his writing-table. He took off the wrapper, and in his eager way fell to reading the first he touched.

It was the first volume of the 'Idols of the Market Place.'

Ten or twelve years before, Mr. Wendover had launched this book into a startled and protesting England. It had been the fruit of his first renewal of contact with English life and English ideas after his return from Berlin. Fresh from the speculative ferment of Germany and the far profaner scepticism of France, he had returned to a society where the first chapter of Genesis and the theory of verbal inspiration were still regarded as valid and important counters on the board of thought. The result had been this book. In it each stronghold of English popular religion had been assailed in turn, at a time when English orthodoxy was a far more formidable thing than it is now.

The Pentateuch, the Prophets, the Gospels, St. Paul, Tradition, the Fathers, Protestantism and Justification by Faith, the Eighteenth Century, the Broad Church Movement, Anglican Theology—the Squire had his say about them all. And while the coolness and frankness of the method sent a shook of indignation and horror through the religious public, the subtle and caustic style, and the epigrams with which the book was strewn, forced both the religious and irreligious public to read, whether they would or no. A storm of controversy rose round the volumes, and some of the keenest observers of English life had said at the time, and maintained since, that the publication of the book had made or marked an epoch.

Robert had lit on those pages in the Essay on the Gospels where the Squire fell to analyzing the evidence for the Resurrection, following up his analysis by an attempt at reconstructing the conditions out of which the belief in 'the legend' arose. Robert began to read vaguely at first, then to hurry on through page after page, still standing, seized at once by the bizarre power of the style, the audacity and range of the treatment.

Not a sound in the house. Outside, the tossing, moaning December night; inside, the faintly crackling fire, the standing figure. Suddenly it was to Robert as though a cruel torturing hand were laid upon his inmost being. His breath failed him; the book slipped out of his grasp; he sank down upon his chair, his head in his hands. Oh, what a desolate, intolerable moment! Over the young idealist soul there swept a dry destroying whirlwind of thought. Elements Gathered from all sources—from his own historical work, from the Squire's book, from the secret, half-conscious recesses of the mind—entered into it, and as it passed it seemed to scorch the heart.

He stayed bowed there a while, then he roused himself with a half-groan, and hastily extinguishing his lamp; he groped his way upstairs to his wife's room. Catherine lay asleep. The child, lost among its white coverings, slept too; there was a dim light over the bed, the books, the pictures. Beside his wife's pillow was a table on which there lay open her little Testament and the 'Imitation' her father had given her. Elsmere sank down beside her, appalled by the contrast between this soft religious peace and that black agony of doubt which still overshadowed him. He knelt there, restraining his breath lest it should wake her, wrestling piteously with himself, crying for pardon, for faith, feeling himself utterly unworthy to touch even the dear hand that lay so near him. But gradually the traditional forces of his life reasserted themselves. The horror lifted. Prayer brought comfort and a passionate, healing self-abasement. 'Master, forgive—defend—purify—' cried the aching heart. '*There is none other that fighteth for us, but only Thou, O God!*'

He did not open the book again. Next morning he put it back into his shelves. If there were any Christian who could affront such an antagonist with a light heart, he felt with a shudder of memory it was not he.

'I have neither learning nor experience enough—yet,' he said to himself slowly as he moved away. 'Of course it can be met, but I must grow, must think—first.'

And of that night's wrestle he said not a word to any living soul. He did penance for it in the tenderest, most secret ways, but he shrank in misery from the thought of revealing it even to Catherine.

CHAPTER XXI

Meanwhile the poor poisoned folk at Mile End lived and apparently throve, in defiance of all the laws of the universe. Robert, as soon as he found that radical measures were for the time hopeless, had applied himself with redoubled energy to making the people use such palliatives as were within their reach, and had preached boiled water and the removal of filth till, as he declared to Catherine, his dreams were one long sanitary nightmare. But he was not confiding enough to believe that the people paid much heed, and he hoped more from a dry hard winter than from any exertion either of his or theirs.

But, alas! with the end of November a season of furious rain set in.

Then Robert began to watch Mile End with anxiety, for so far every outbreak of illness there had followed upon unusual damp. But the rains passed leaving behind them no worse result than the usual winter crop of lung ailments and rheumatism, and he breathed again.

Christmas came and went, and with the end of December the wet weather returned. Day after day rolling masses of southwest cloud came up from the Atlantic and wrapped the whole country in rain, which reminded Catherine of her Westmoreland rain more than any she had yet seen in the South. Robert accused her of liking it for that reason, but she shook her head with a sigh, declaring that it was 'nothing without the peaks.'

One afternoon she was shutting the door of the school behind her, and stepping out on the road skirting the green—the bedabbled wintry green— when she saw Robert emerging from the Mile End lane. She crossed over to him, wondering, as she neared him, that he seemed to take no notice of her. He was striding along, his wideawake over his eyes, and so absorbed that she had almost touched him before he saw her.

'Darling, is that you? Don't stop me, I am going to take the pony-carriage in for Meyrick. I have just come back from that accursed place; three cases of diphtheria in one house, Sharland's wife—and two others down with fever.'

She made a horrified exclamation.

'It will spread,' he said gloomily, 'I know it will. I never saw the children look such a ghastly crew before. Well, I must go for Meyrick and a nurse, and we must isolate and make a fight for it.'

In a few days the diphtheria epidemic reached terrible proportion's. There had been one death, others were expected, and soon Robert in his brief hours at home could find no relief in anything, so heavy was the oppression of the day's memories. At first Catherine for the child's sake kept away; but the little Mary was weaned, had a good Scotch nurse, was in every way thriving, and after a day or two Catherine's craving to help, to be with Robert in his trouble was too strong to be withstood. But she dared not go backward and forward between her baby and the diphtheritic children. So she bethought herself of Mrs. Elsmere's servant, old Martha, who was still inhabiting Mrs. Elsmere's cottage till a tenant could be found for it, and doing good service meanwhile as an occasional parish nurse. The baby and its nurse went over to the cottage. Catherine carried the child there, wrapped close in maternal arms, and leaving her on old Martha's lap, went back to Robert.

Then she and he devoted themselves to a hand-to-hand fight with the epidemic. At the climax of it, there were about twenty children down with it in different stages, and seven cases of fever. They had two hospital nurses; one of the better cottages, turned into a sanatorium, accommodated the worst cases under the nurses, and Robert and Catherine, directed by them and the doctors, took the responsibility of the rest, he helping to nurse the boys and she the girls. Of the fever cases Sharland's wife was the worst. A feeble creature at all times, it seemed almost impossible she could weather through. But day after day passed, and by dint of incessant nursing she still lived. A youth of twenty, the main support of a mother and five or six younger children, was also desperately ill. Robert hardly ever had him out of his thoughts, and the boy's doglike affection for the Rector, struggling with his deathly weakness, was like a perpetual exemplification of Ahriman and Ormuzd—the power of life struggling with the power of death.

It was a fierce fight. Presently it seemed to the husband and wife as though the few daily hours spent at the rectory were mere halts between successive acts of battle with the plague-fiend—a more real and grim Grendel of the Marshes—for the lives of children. Catherine could always sleep in these intervals, quietly and dreamlessly; Robert very soon could only sleep by the help of some prescription of old Meyrick's. On all occasions of strain since his boyhood there had been signs in him of a certain lack of constitutional hardness which his mother knew very well, but which his wife was only just beginning to recognize. However, he laughed to scorn any attempt to restrain his constant goings and comings, or those hours of night-nursing, in which, as the hospital nurses were the first to admit, no one was so successful as the Rector. And when he stood up on Sundays to preach in Murewell Church, the worn and spiritual look of the man, and the knowledge warm at each heart of those before him of how the Rector not only talked but lived, carried every word home.

This strain upon all the moral and physical forces, however, strangely enough, came to Robert as a kind of relief. It broke through a tension of brain which of late had become an oppression. And for both him and Catherine these dark times had moments of intensest joy, points of white light illuminating heaven and earth.

There were cloudy nights—wet, stormy January nights—when sometimes it happened to them to come back both together from the hamlet, Robert carrying a lantern, Catherine clothed in waterproof from head to foot, walking beside him, the rays flashing now on her face, now on the wooded sides of the lane, while the wind howled through the dark vault of branches overhead. And then, as they talked or were silent, suddenly a sense of the intense blessedness of this comradeship of theirs would rise like a flood in the man's heart, and he would fling his free arm round her, forcing her to stand a moment in the January night and storm while he said to her words of passionate gratitude, of faith in an immortal union reaching beyond change or deaths lost in a kiss which was a sacrament. Then there were the moments when they saw their child, held high in Martha's arms at the window, and leaping toward her mother; the moments when one pallid, sickly being after another was pronounced out of danger; and by the help of them the weeks passed away.

Nor were they left without help from outside. Lady Helen Varley no sooner heard the news than she hurried over. Robert on his way one morning from one cottage to another saw her pony-carriage in the lane. He hastened up to her before she could dismount.

'No, Lady Helen, you mustn't come here,' he said to her peremptorily, as she held out her hand.

'Oh, Mr. Elsmere, let me. My boy is in town with his grandmother. Let me just go through, at any rate, and see what I can send you.'

Robert shook his head, smiling. A common friend of theirs and hers had once described this little lady to Elsmere by a French sentence which originally applied to the Duchesse de Choiseul. 'Une charmante petite fée sortie d'un oeuf enchanté!'—so it ran. Certainly, as Elsmere looked down upon her now, fresh from those squalid death-stricken hovels behind him, he was brought more abruptly than ever upon the contrasts of life. Lady Helen wore a green velvet and fur mantle, in the production of which even

Worth had felt some pride; a little green velvet bonnet perched on her fair hair; one tiny hand, ungloved, seemed ablaze with diamonds; there were opals and diamonds somewhere at her throat, gleaming among her sables. But she wore her jewels as carelessly as she wore her high birth, her quaint, irregular prettiness, or the one or two brilliant gifts which made her sought after wherever she went. She loved her opals as she loved all bright things; if it pleased her to wear them in the morning she wore them; and in five minutes she was capable of making the sourest Puritan forget to frown on her and them. To Robert she always seemed the quintessence of breeding, of aristocracy at their best. All her freaks, her sallies, her absurdities even, were graceful. At her freest and gayest there were things in her—restraints, reticences, perceptions—which implied behind her generations of rich, happy, important people, with ample leisure to cultivate all the more delicate niceties of social feeling and relation. Robert was often struck by the curious differences between her and Rose. Rose was far the handsome; she was at least as clever; and she had a strong imperious will where Lady Helen had only impulses and sympathies and *engouements*. But Rose belonged to the class which struggles, where each individual depends on himself and knows it. Lady Helen had never struggled for anything—all the best things of the world were hers so easily that she hardly gave them a thought; or rather, what she had gathered without pain she held so lightly, she dispensed so lavishly, that men's eyes followed her, fluttering through life, with much the same feeling as was struck from Clough's radical hero by the peerless Lady Maria:—

> *Live, be lovely, forget us, be beautiful, even to proudness,*
>
> *Even for their poor sakes whose happiness is to behold you;*
>
> *Live, be uncaring, be joyous, be sumptuous; only be lovely!*

'Uncaring,' however, little Lady Helen never was. If she was a fairy, she was a fairy all heart, all frank, foolish smiles and tears.

'No, Lady Helen—no,' Robert said again. 'This is no place for you, and we are getting on capitally.'

She pouted a little.

'I believe you and Mrs. Elsmere are just killing yourselves all in a corner, with no one to see,' she said indignantly. 'If you won't let me see, I shall send Sir Harry. But who'—and her brown fawn's eyes ran startled over the cottages before her—'who, Mr. Elsmere, does this *dreadful* place belong to?'

'Mr. Wendover,' said Robert shortly.

'Impossible!' she cried incredulously. 'Why, I wouldn't ask one of my dogs to sleep there,' and she pointed to the nearest hovel, whereof the walls were tottering outward, the thatch was falling to pieces, and the windows were mended with anything that came handy—rags, paper, or the crown of an old hat.

'No, you would be ill-advised' said Robert, looking with a bitter little smile at the sleek dachshund that sat blinking beside its mistress.

'But what is the agent about?'

Then Robert told her the story, not mincing his words. Since the epidemic had begun, all that sense of imaginative attraction which had been reviving in him toward the Squire had been simply blotted out by a fierce heat of indignation. When he thought of Mr. Wendover now, he thought of him as the man to whom in strict truth it was owing that helpless children died in choking torture. All that agony, of wrath and pity he had gone through in the last ten days sprang to his lips now as he talked to Lady Helen, and poured itself into his words.

'Old Meyrick and I have taken things into our own hands now,' he said at last briefly. 'We have already made two cottages fairly habitable. To-morrow the inspector comes. I told the people yesterday I wouldn't be bound by my promise a day longer. He must put the screw on Henslowe, and if Henslowe dawdles, why we shall just drain and repair and sink for a well, ourselves. I can find the money somehow. At present we get all our water from one of the farms on the brow.'

'Money!' said Lady Helen impulsively, her looks warm with sympathy for the pale, harassed young rector. 'Sir Harry shall send you as much as you want. And anything else—blankets—coals?'

Out came her notebooks and Robert was drawn into a list. Then, full of joyfulness at being allowed to help, she gathered up her reins, she nodded her pretty little head at him, and was just starting off her ponies at full speed, equally eager 'to tell Harry' and to ransack Churton for the stores required, when it occurred to her to pull up again.

'Oh, Mr. Elsmere, my aunt, Lady Charlotte, does nothing but talk about your sister-in-law. *Why* did you keep her all to yourself? Is it kind, is it neighborly, to have such a wonder to stay with you and let nobody share?'

'A wonder?' said Robert, amused. 'Rose plays the violin very well, but—'

'As if relations ever saw one in proper perspective!' exclaimed Lady Helen. 'My aunt wants to be allowed to have her in town next season if you will all let her. I think she would find it fun. Aunt Charlotte knows all the world and his wife. And if I'm there, and Miss Leyburn will let me make friends with her, why, you know, *I* can just protect her a little from Aunt Charlotte?'

The little laughing face bent forward again; Robert, smiling, raised his hat, and the ponies whirled her off. In anybody else Elsmere would have thought all this effusion insincere or patronizing. But Lady Helen was the most spontaneous of mortals, and the only highborn woman he had ever met who was really, and not only apparently, free from the 'nonsense of rank.' Robert shrewdly suspected Lady Charlotte's social tolerance to be a mere varnish. But this little person, and her favorite brother Hugh, to judge from the accounts of him, must always have found life too romantic, too wildly and delightfully interesting from top to bottom, to be measured by any but romantic standards.

Next day Sir Harry Varley, a great burly country squire, who adored his wife, kept the hounds, owned a model estate, and thanked God every morning that he was an Englishman, rode over to Mile End. Robert, who had just been round the place with the inspector and was dead tired, had only energy to show him a few of the worst enormities. Sir Harry, leaving a check behind him, rode off with a discharge of strong language, at which Robert, clergyman as he was, only grimly smiled.

A few days later Mr. Wendover's crimes as a landowner, his agent's brutality, young Elsmere's devotion, and the horrors of the Mile End outbreak, were in everybody's mouth. The county was roused. The Radical newspaper came out on the Saturday with a flaming article; Robert, much to his annoyance, found himself the local hero; and money began to come in to him freely.

On the Monday morning Henslowe appeared on the scene with an army of workmen. A racy communication from the inspector had reached him two days before, so had a copy of the 'Churton Advertiser.' He had spent Sunday in a drinking bout turning over all possible plans of vengeance and evasion. Toward the evening, however, his wife, a gaunt clever Scotchwoman, who saw ruin before them, and had on occasion an even sharper tongue than her husband, managed to capture the supplies of brandy in the house and effectually conceal them. Then she waited for the moment of collapse which came on toward morning, and with her hands on her hips she poured into him a volley of home-truths which not even Sir Harry Varley could have bettered. Henslowe's nerve gave way. He went out at daybreak, white and sullen, to look for workmen.

Robert, standing on the step of a cottage, watched him give his orders, and took vigilant note of their substance. They embodied the inspector's directions, and the Rector was satisfied. Henslowe was obliged to pass him on his way to another group of houses. At first he affected not to see the Rector, then suddenly Elsmere was conscious that the man's bloodshot eyes were on him. Such a look! If hate could have killed, Elsmere would have fallen where he stood. Yet the man's hand mechanically moved to his hat, as though the spell of his wife's harangue were still potent over his shaking muscles.

Robert took no notice whatever of the salutation. He stood calmly watching till Henslowe disappeared into the last house. Then he called one of the agent's train, heard what was to be done, gave a sharp nod of assent, and turned on his heel. So far so good: the servant had been made to feel, but he wished it had been the master. Oh, those three little emaciated creatures whose eyes he had closed, whose clammy hands he had held to the last!—what reckoning should be asked for their undeserved torments when the Great Account came to be made up?

Meanwhile not a sound apparently of all this reached the Squire in the sublime solitude of Murewell. A fortnight had passed. Henslowe had been conquered, the county had rushed to Elsmere's help, and neither he nor Mrs. Darcy had made a sign. Their life was so abnormal that it was perfectly possible they had heard nothing. Elsmere wondered when they *would* hear.

The Rector's chief help and support all through had been old Meyrick. The parish doctor had been in bed with rheumatism when the epidemic broke out, and Robert, feeling it a comfort to be rid of him, had thrown the whole business into the hands of Meyrick and his son. This son was nominally his father's junior partner, but as he was, besides, a young and brilliant M.D. fresh from a great hospital, and his father was just a poor old general practitioner, with the barest qualification and only forty years' experience to recommend him, it will easily be imagined that the subordination was purely nominal. Indeed young Meyrick was fast ousting his father in all directions, and the neighborhood, which had so far found itself unable either to enter or to quit this mortal scene without old Meyrick's assistance, was beginning to send notes to the house in Charton High Street, whereon the superscription 'Dr. *Edward* Meyrick' was underlined with ungrateful emphasis. The father took his deposition very quietly. Only on Murewell Hall would he allow no trespassing, and so long as his son left him undisturbed there, he took his effacement in other quarters with perfect meekness.

Young Elsmere's behavior to him, however, at a time when all the rest of the Churton world was beginning to hold him cheap and let him see it, had touched the old man's heart, and he was the Rector's slave in this Mile End business. Edward Meyrick would come whirling in and out of the hamlet once a day. Robert was seldom sorry to see the back of him. His attainments, of course, were useful, but his cocksureness was irritating, and his manner to his father, abominable. The father, on the other hand, came over in the shabby pony-cart he had driven for the last forty years, and having himself no press of business, would spend hours with the Rector over the cases, giving them an infinity of patient watching, and amusing Robert by the cautious hostility he would allow himself every now and then toward his souls newfangled devices.

At first Meyrick showed himself fidgety as to the Squire. Had he been seen, been heard from? He received Robert's sharp negatives with long sighs, but Robert clearly saw that, like the rest of the world, he was too much afraid of Mr. Wendover to go and beard him. Some months before, as it happened, Elsmere had told him the story of his encounter with the Squire, and had been a good deal moved and surprised by the old man's concern.

One day, about three weeks from the beginning of the outbreak, when the state of things in the hamlet was beginning decidedly to mend, Meyrick arrived for his morning round, much preoccupied. He hurried his work a little, and after it was done asked Robert to walk up the road with him.

'I have seen the Squire, sir,' he said, turning on his companion with a certain excitement.

Robert flushed.

'Have you?' he replied with his hands behind him, and a world of expression in his sarcastic voice.

'You misjudge him! You misjudge him, Mr. Elsmere!' the old man said tremulously. 'I told you he could know of this business—and he didn't! He has been in town part of the time, and down here, how is he to know anything? He sees nobody. That man Henslowe, sir, must be a real *bad* fellow.'

'Don't abuse the man,' said Robert, looking up. 'It's not worth while, when you can say your mind of the master.'

Old Meyrick sighed.

'Well,' said Robert, after a moment, his lip drawn and quivering, 'you told him the story, I suppose? Seven deaths, is it, by now? Well, what sort of impression did these unfortunate accidents'—and he smiled—'produce?'

'He talked of sending money,' said Meyrick doubtfully; he said he would have Henslowe up and inquire. He seemed put about and annoyed. Oh, Mr. Elsmere, you think too hardly of the Squire, that you do!'

They strolled on together in silence. Robert was not inclined to discuss the matter. But old Meyrick seemed to be laboring under some suppressed emotion, and presently he began upon his own experiences as a doctor of the Wendover family. He had already broached the subject more or less vaguely with Robert. Now, however, he threw his medical reserve, generally his strongest characteristic, to the winds. He insisted on telling his companion, who listened reluctantly, the whole miserable and ghastly story of the old Squire's suicide. He described the heir's summons, his arrival just in time for the last scene with all its horrors, and that mysterious condition of the Squire for some months afterward, when no one, not even Mrs. Darcy, had been admitted to the Hall, and old Meyrick, directed at intervals by a great London doctor, had been the only spectator of Roger Wendover's physical and mental breakdown, the only witness of that dark consciousness of inherited fatality which at that period of his life not even the Squire's iron will had been able wholly to conceal.

Robert, whose attention was inevitably roused after a while, found himself with some curiosity realizing the Squire from another man's totally different point of view. Evidently Meyrick had seen him at such moments as wring from the harshest nature whatever grains of tenderness, of pity, or of natural human weakness may be in it. And it was clear, too, that the Squire, conscious perhaps of a shared secret, and feeling a certain soothing influence in the *naïveté* and simplicity of the old man's sympathy, had allowed himself at times, in the years succeeding that illness of his, an amount of unbending in Meyrick's presence, such as probably no other mortal had ever witnessed in him since his earliest youth.

And yet how childish the old man's whole mental image of the Squire was after all! What small account it made of the subtleties, the gnarled intricacies and contradictions of such a character! Horror at his father's end, and dread of a like fate for himself! Robert did not know very much of the Squire, but he knew enough to feel sure that this confiding, indulgent theory of Meyrick's was ludicrously far from the mark as an adequate explanation of Mr. Wendover's later life.

Presently Meyrick became aware of the sort of tacit resistance which his companion's mind was opposing to his own. He dropped the wandering narrative he was busy upon with a sigh.

'Ah well, I dare say it's hard, it's hard,' he said with patient acquiescence in his voice, 'to believe a man can't help himself. I dare say we doctors get

to muddle up right and wrong. But if ever there was a man sick in mind—
for all his book learning they talk about—and sick in soul, that man is the
Squire.'

Robert looked at him with a softer expression. There was a new dignity
about the simple old man. The old-fashioned deference, which had never let
him forget in speaking to Robert that he was speaking to a man of family,
and which showed itself in all sorts of antiquated locutions which were a
torment to his son, had given way to something still more deeply ingrained.
His gaunt figure, with the stoop, and the spectacles, and the long straight
hair—like the figure of a superannuated schoolmaster—assumed, as he
turned again to his younger companion, something of authority, something
almost of stateliness.

'Ah, Mr. Elsmere,' he said, laying his shrunk hand on the younger man's
sleeve and speaking with emotion, 'you're very good to the poor. We're all
proud of you—you and your good lady. But when you were coming, and I
heard tell all about you, I thought of my poor Squire, and I said to myself,
"That young man'll be good to *him*. The Squire will make friends with him,
and Mr. Elsmere will have a good wife—and there'll be children born to
him—and the Squire will take an interest—and—and—maybe——"

The old man paused. Robert grasped his hand silently.

'And there was something in the way between you,' the speaker went
on, starting. 'I dare say you were quite right—quite right. I can't judge.
Only there are ways of doing a thing. And it was a last chance; and now
it's missed—it's missed. Ah! It's no good talking; he has a heart—he has!
Many's the kind thing he's done in old days for me and mine—I'll never
forget them! But all these last few years—oh, I know, I know. You can't go
and shut your heart up, and fly in the face of all the duties the Lord laid
on you, without losing yourself and setting the Lord against you. But it is
pitiful, Mr. Elsmere, it's pitiful!'

It seemed to Robert suddenly as though there was a Divine breath
passing through the wintry, lane and through the shaking voice of the
old man. Beside the spirit looking out of those wrinkled eyes, his own hot
youth, its justest resentments, its most righteous angers, seemed crude,
harsh, inexcusable.

'Thank you, Meyrick, thank you, and God bless you! Don't imagine I
will forget a word you have said to me.'

The Rector shook the hand he held warmly twice over, a gentle smile
passed over Meyrick's aging face, and they parted.

That night it fell to Robert to sit up after midnight with John Allwood, the youth of twenty whose case had been a severer tax on the powers of the little nursing staff than perhaps any other. Mother and neighbors were worn out, and it was difficult to spare a hospital nurse for long together from the diphtheria cases. Robert, therefore, had insisted during the preceding week on taking alternate nights with one of the nurses. During the first hours before midnight he slept soundly on a bed made up in the ground-floor room of the little sanatorium. Then at twelve the nurse called him, and he went out, his eyes still heavy with sleep, into a still, frosty winter's night.

After so much rain, so much restlessness of wind and cloud, the silence and the starry calm of it were infinitely welcome. The sharp cold air cleared his brain and braced his nerves, and by the time he reached the cottage whither he was bound, he was broad awake. He opened the door softly, passed through the lower room, crowded with sleeping children, climbed the narrow stairs as noiselessly as possible, and found himself in a garret, faintly lit, a bed in one corner, and a woman sitting beside it. The woman glided away, the Rector looked carefully at the table of instructions hanging over the bed, assured himself that wine and milk and beef essence and medicines were ready to his hand, put out his watch on the wooden table near the bed, and sat him down to his task. The boy was sleeping the sleep of weakness. Food was to be given every half hour, and in this perpetual impulse to the system lay his only chance.

The Rector had his Greek Testament with him, and could just read it by the help of the dim light. But after a while, as the still hours passed on, it dropped on to his knee, and he sat thinking—endlessly thinking. The young laborer lay motionless beside him, the lines of the long emaciated frame showing through the bedclothes. The night-light flickered on the broken, discolored ceiling; every now and then a mouse scratched in the plaster; the mother's heavy breathing came from the next room; sometimes a dog barked or an owl cried outside. Otherwise deep silence, such silence as drives the soul back upon itself.

Elsmere was conscious of a strange sense of moral expansion. The stern judgments, the passionate condemnations which his nature housed so painfully, seemed lifted from it. The soul breathed an 'ampler æther, a diviner air.' Oh! the mysteries of life and character, the subtle, inexhaustible claims of pity! The problems which hang upon our being here; its mixture of elements; the pressure of its inexorable physical environment; the relations of mind to body, of man's poor will to this tangled tyrannous life—it was along these old, old lines his thought went painfully groping and always at intervals it came back to the Squire, pondering, seeking to understand, a new soberness, a new humility and patience entering in.

And yet it was not Meyrick's facts exactly that had brought this about. Robert thought them imperfect, only half true. Rather was it the spirit of love, of infinite forbearance in which the simpler, duller nature had declared itself that had appealed to him, nay, reproached him.

Then these thoughts led him on further and further from man to God, from human defect to the Eternal Perfectness. Never once during those hours did Elsmere's hand fail to perform its needed service to the faint sleeper beside him, and yet that night was one long dream and strangeness to him, nothing real anywhere but consciousness, and God its source; the soul attacked every now and then by phantom stabs of doubt, of bitter, brief misgiving, as the barriers of sense between it and the eternal enigma grew more and more transparent, wrestling a while, and then prevailing. And each golden moment of certainty, of conquering faith, seemed to Robert in some sort a gift from Catherine's hand. It was she who led him through the shades; it was her voice murmuring in his ear.

When the first gray dawn began to creep in slowly perceptible waves into the room, Elsmere felt as though not hours but fears of experience lay between him and the beginnings of his watch.

'It is by these moments we should date our lives' he murmured to himself as he rose: 'they are the only real landmarks.'

It was eight o'clock, and the nurse who was to relieve him had come. The results of the night for his charge were good: the strength had been maintained, the pulse was firmer, the temperature lower. The boy, throwing off his drowsiness, lay watching the Rector's face as he talked in an undertone to the nurse, his haggard eyes full of a dumb, friendly wistfulness. When Robert bent over him to say good-by, this expression brightened into something more positive, and Robert left him, feeling at last that there was a promise of life in his look and touch.

In, another moment he had stepped out into the January morning. It was clear and still as the night had been. In the east there was a pale promise of sun; the reddish-brown trunks of the fir woods had just caught it and rose faintly in glowing in endless vistas and colonnades one behind the other. The flooded river itself rushed through the bridge as full and turbid as before, but all the other water surfaces had gleaming films of ice. The whole ruinous place had a clean, almost a festal air under the touch of the frost, while on the side of the hill leading to Murewell, tree rose above tree, the delicate network of their wintry twigs and branches set against stretches of frost-whitened grass, till finally they climbed into the pale all-completing blue. In a copse close at hand there were woodcutters at work, and piles of gleaming laths shining through the underwood. Robins hopped along the frosty road, and as he walked on through the houses toward the bridge, Robert's quick ear distinguished that most wintry of all sounds—the cry of a flock of field-fares passing overhead.

As he neared the bridge he suddenly caught sight of a figure upon it, the figure of a man wrapped in a large Inverness cloak, leaning against the stone parapet. With a start he recognized the Squire.

He went up to him without an instant's slackening of his steady step. The Squire heard the sound of someone coming, turned, and saw the Rector.

'I am glad to see you here, Mr. Wendover,' said Robert, stopping and holding out his hand. 'I meant to have come to talk to you about this place this morning. I ought to have come before.'

He spoke gently, and quite simply, almost as if they had parted the day before. The Squire touched his hand for an instant.

'You may not, perhaps, be aware, Mr. Elsmere,' he said, endeavoring to speak with all his old hauteur, while his heavy lips twitched nervously, 'that, for one reason and another, I knew nothing of the epidemic here till yesterday, when Meyrick told me.'

'I heard from Mr. Meyrick that it was so. As you are here now, Mr. Wendover, and I am in no great hurry to get home, may I take you through and show you the people?'

The Squire at last looked at him straight—at the face worn and pale, yet still so extraordinarily youthful, in which something of the solemnity and high emotion of the night seemed to be still lingering.

'Are you just come?' he said abruptly, 'or are you going back?'

'I have been here through the night, sitting up with one of the fever cases. It's hard work for the nurses and the relations sometimes, without help.'

The Squire moved on mechanically toward the village, and Robert moved beside him.

'And Mrs. Elsmere?'

'Mrs. Elsmere was here most of yesterday. She used to stay the night when the diphtheria was at its worst; but there are only four anxious cases left, the rest all convalescent.'

The Squire said no more, and they turned into the lane, where the ice lay thick in the deep ruts, and on either hand curls of smoke rose into the clear cold sky. The Squire looked about him with eyes which no detail escaped. Robert, without a word of comment, pointed out this feature and that, showed where Henslowe had begun repairs, where the new well was to be, what the water-supply had been till now, drew the Squire's attention to the roofs, the pigstyes, the drainage, or rather complete absence of drainage, and all in the dry voice of someone going through a catalogue. Word had already fled like wildfire through the hamlet that the Squire was there. Children and adults, a pale emaciated crew, poured out into the wintry air to look. The Squire knit his brows with annoyance as the little crowd in the lane grew. Robert took no notice.

Presently he pushed open the door of the house where he had spent the night. In the kitchen a girl of sixteen was clearing away the various nondescript heaps on which the family had slept, and was preparing breakfast. The Squire looked at the floor,—

'I thought I understood from Henslowe,' he muttered, as though to himself, 'that there were no mud floors left on the estate—'

'There are only three houses in Mile End without them; said Robert, catching what he said.

They went upstairs, and the mother stood open-eyed while the Squire's restless look gathered in the details of the room, the youth's face as he lay back on his pillows, whiter than they, exhausted and yet refreshed by the sponging with vinegar and water which the mother had just been administering to him; the bed, the gaps in the worm-eaten boards, the holes in the roof where the plaster bulged inward, as though a shake would bring it down; the coarse china shepherdesses on the mantelshelf, and the flowers which Catherine had put there the day before. He asked a few questions, said an abrupt word or two to the mother, and they tramped downstairs again and into the street. Then Robert took him across to the little improvised hospital, saying to him on the threshold, with a moment's hesitation,—

'As you know, for adults there is not much risk, but there is always some risk—'

A peremptory movement of the Squire's hand stopped him, and they went in. In the downstairs room were half-a-dozen convalescents, pale, shadowy creatures, four of them under ten, sitting up in their little cots, each of them with a red flannel jacket drawn from Lady Helen's stores, and enjoying the breakfast which a nurse in white cap and apron had just brought them. Upstairs in a room from which a lath-and-plaster partition had been removed, and which had been adapted, warmed and ventilated by various contrivances to which Robert and Meyrick had devoted their practical minds, were the 'four anxious cases.' One of them, a little creature of six, one of Sharland's black-eyed children, was sitting up, supported by the nurse, and coughing, its little life away. As soon as he saw it, Robert's step quickened. He forgot the Squire altogether. He came and stood by the bedside, rigidly still, for he could do nothing, but his whole soul absorbed in that horrible struggle for air. How often he had seen it now, and never without the same wild sense of revolt and protest! At last the hideous membrane was loosened, the child got relief and lay back white and corpselike, but with a pitiful momentary relaxation of the drawn lines on its little brow. Robert stooped and kissed the damp tiny hand. The child's eyes remained shut, but the fingers made a feeble effort to close on his.

'Mr. Elsmere,' said the nurse, a motherly body, looking at him with friendly admonition, 'if you don't go home and rest you'll be ill too, and I'd like to know who'll be the better for that?'

'How many deaths?' asked the Squire abruptly, touching Elsmere's arm, and so reminding Robert of his existence. 'Meyrick spoke of deaths.'

He stood near the door, but his eyes were fixed on the little bed, on the half-swooning child.

'Seven,' said Robert, turning upon him. 'Five of diphtheria, two of fever. That little one will go, too.'

'Horrible!' said the Squire under his breath, and then moved to the door.

The two men went downstairs in perfect silence. Below, in the convalescent room, the children were capable of smiles, and of quick, coquettish beckonings to the Rector to come and make game with them as usual. But he could only kiss his hand to them and escape, for there was more to do.

He took the Squire through all the remaining fever cases, and into several of the worst cottages—Milsom's among them—and when it was all over they emerged into the lane again, near the bridge. There was still a crowd of children and women hanging about, watching eagerly for the Squire, whom many of them had never seen at all, and about whom various myths had gradually formed themselves in the country-side. The Squire walked away from them hurriedly, followed by Robert, and again they halted on the centre of the bridge. A horse led by a groom was being walked up and down on a flat piece of road just beyond.

It was an awkward moment. Robert never forgot the thrill of it, or the association of wintry sunshine streaming down upon a sparkling world of ice and delicate woodland and foam-flecked river.

The squire turned toward him irresolutely; his sharply-cut wrinkled lips opening and closing again. Then he held out his hand: 'Mr. Elsmere, I did you a wrong—I did this place and its people a wrong. In my view, regret for the past is useless. Much of what has occurred here is plainly irreparable; I will think what can be done for the future. As for my relation to you, it rests with you to say whether it can be amended. I recognize that you have just cause of complaint.'

What invincible pride there was in the man's very surrender! But Elsmere was not repelled by it. He knew that in their hour together the Squire had *felt*. His soul had lost its bitterness. The dead and their wrong were with God.

He took the Squire's outstretched hand, grasping it cordially, a pure, unworldly dignity in his whole look and bearing.

'Let us be friends, Mr. Wendover. It will be a great comfort to us—my wife and me. Will you remember us both very kindly to Mrs. Darcy?'

Commonplace words, but words that made an epoch in the life of both. In another minute the Squire, on horse-back, was trotting along the side road leading to the Hall, and Robert was speeding home to Catherine as fast as his long legs could carry him.

She was waiting for him on the steps, shading her eyes against the unwonted sun. He kissed her with the spirits of a boy and told her all, his news.

Catherine listened bewildered, not knowing what to say or how all at once to forgive, to join Robert in forgetting. But that strange spiritual glow about him was not to be withstood. She threw her arms about him at last with a half sob,—

'Oh, Robert—yes! Dear Robert—thank God!'

'Never think any more,' he said at last, leading her in from the little hall, 'of What has been, only of what shall be! Oh, Catherine, give me some tea; and never did I see anything so tempting as that armchair.'

'He sank down into it, and when she put his breakfast beside him she saw with a start that he was fast asleep. The wife stood and watched him, the signs of fatigue round eyes and mouth, the placid expression, and her face was soft with tenderness and joy. Of course—of course, even that hard man must love him. Who could help it? My Robert!'

And so now in this disguise, now in that, the supreme hour of Catherine's life stole on and on toward her.

CHAPTER XXII

As may be imagined, the 'Churton Advertiser' did not find its way to Murewell. It was certainly no pressure of social disapproval that made the Squire go down to Mile End in that winter's dawn. The county might talk, or the local press might harangue, till Doomsday, and Mr. Wendover would either know nothing or care less.

Still his interview with Meyrick in the park after his return from a week in town, whither he had gone to see some old Berlin friends, had been a shock to him. A man may play the intelligent recluse, may refuse to fit his life to his neighbors' notions as much as you please, and still find death, especially death for which he has some responsibility, as disturbing a fact as the rest of us.

He went home in much irritable discomfort. It seemed to him probably that fortune need not have been so eager to put him in the wrong. To relieve his mind he sent for Henslowe, and in an interview, the memory of which sent a shiver through the agent to the end of his days, he let it be seen that though it did not for the moment suit him to dismiss the man who had brought this upon him, that man's reign in any true sense was over.

But afterward the Squire was still restless. What was astir in him was not so much pity or remorse as certain instincts of race which still survived under the strange super-structure of manners he had built upon them. It may be the part of a gentlemen and a scholar to let the agent whom you have interposed between yourself and a boorish peasantry have a free hand; but, after all, the estate is yours, and to expose the rector of the parish to all sorts of avoidable risks in the pursuit of his official duty by reason of the gratuitous filth of your property, is an act of doubtful breeding. The Squire in his most rough-and-tumble days at Berlin had always felt himself the grandee as well as the student. He abhorred sentimentalism, but neither did he choose to cut an unseemly figure in his own eyes.

After a night, therefore, less tranquil or less meditative than usual, he rose early and sallied forth at one of those unusual hours he generally chose for walking. The thing must be put right somehow, and at once, with as little waste of time and energy as possible, and Henslowe had shown himself not to be trusted; so telling a servant to follow him, the Squire had made his way with difficulty to a place he had not seen for years.

Then had followed the unexpected and unwelcome apparition of the Rector. The Squire did not want to be impressed by the young man; did not want to make friends with him. No doubt his devotion had served his own purposes. Still Mr. Wendover was one of the subtlest living judges of character when he pleased, and his enforced progress through these hovels with Elsmere had not exactly softened him, but had filled him with a curious contempt for his own hastiness of judgment.

'History would be inexplicable after all without the honest fanatic,' he said to himself on the way home. 'I suppose I had forgotten it. There is nothing like a dread of being bored for blunting your psychological instinct.'

In the course of the day he sent off a letter to the Rector intimating in the very briefest, dryest way that the cottages should be rebuilt on a different site as soon as possible, and enclosing a liberal contribution toward the expenses incurred in fighting the epidemic. When the letter was gone he drew his books toward him with a sound which was partly disgust, partly relief. This annoying business had wretchedly interrupted him, and his concessions left him mainly conscious of a strong nervous distaste for the idea of any fresh interview with young Elsmere. He had got his money and his apology; let him be content.

However, next morning after breakfast, Mr. Wendover once more saw his study door open to admit the tall figure of the Rector. The note and check had reached Robert late the night before, and, true to his new-born determination to make the best of the Squire, he had caught up his wideawake at the first opportunity and walked off to the Hall to acknowledge the gift in person. The interview opened as awkwardly as it was possible, and with their former conversation on the same spot fresh in their minds both men spent a sufficiently difficult ten minutes. The Squire was asking himself, indeed, impatiently, all the time, whether he could possibly be forced in the future to put up with such an experience again, and Robert found his host, if less sarcastic than before, certainly as impenetrable as ever.

At last, however, the Mile End matter was exhausted, and then Robert, as good luck would have it, turned his longing eyes on the Squire's books, especially on the latest volumes of a magnificent German *Weltgeschichte* lying near his elbow, which he had coveted for months without being able to conquer his conscience sufficiently to become the possessor of it. He took it up with an exclamation of delight, and a quiet critical remark that exactly hit the value and scope of the book. The Squire's eyebrows went up, and the corners of his mouth slackened visibly. Half an hour later the two men, to the amazement of Mrs. Darcy, who was watching them from the drawing-room window, walked back to the park gates together, and what Robert's nobility and beauty of character would never have won him, though he had worn himself to death in the service of the poor and the tormented under the Squire's eyes, a chance coincidence of intellectual interest had won him almost in a moment.

The Squire walked back to the house under a threatening sky, his mackintosh cloak wrapped about him, his arms folded, his mind full of an unwonted excitement.

The sentiment of long-past days—days in Berlin, in Paris, where conversations such as that he had just passed through were the daily relief and reward of labor, was stirring in him. Occasionally he had endeavored to import the materials for them from the Continent, from London. But as a matter of fact, it was years since he had had any such talk as this with an Englishman on English ground, and he suddenly realized that he had been unwholesomely solitary, and that for the scholar there is no nerve stimulus like that of an occasional interchange of ideas with some one acquainted with his *Fach*.

'Who would ever have thought of discovering instincts and aptitudes of such a kind in this long-legged optimist?' The Squire shrugged his shoulders as he thought of the attempt involved in such a personality to combine both worlds, the world of action and the world of thought. Absurd! Of course, ultimately one or other must go to the wall.

Meanwhile, what a ludicrous waste of time and opportunity that he and this man should have been at cross-purposes like this! 'Why the deuce couldn't he have given some rational account of himself to begin with!' thought the Squire irritably, forgetting, of course, who it was that had wholly denied him the opportunity. 'And then the sending back of those books: what a piece of idiocy!'

Granted an historical taste in this young parson, it was a curious chance, Mr. Wendover reflected, that in his choice of a subject he should just have fallen on the period of the later Empire—of the passage from the old-world to the new, where the Squire was a master. The Squire fell to thinking of the kind of knowledge implied in his remarks, of the stage he seemed to have reached, and then to cogitating as to the books he must be now in want of. He went back to his library, ran over the shelves, picking out volumes here and there with an unwonted glow and interest all the while. He sent for a case, and made a youth who sometimes acted as his secretary pack them. And still as he went back to his own work new names would occur to him, and full of the scholar's avaricious sense of the shortness of time, he would shake his head and frown over the three months which young Elsmere had already passed, grappling with problems like Teutonic Arianism, the spread of Monasticism in Gaul, and Heaven knows what besides, half a mile from the man and the library which could have supplied him with the best help to be got in England, unbenefited by either! Mile End was obliterated, and the annoyance, of the morning forgotten.

The next day was Sunday, a wet January Sunday, raw and sleety, the frost breaking up on all sides and flooding the roads with mire.

Robert, rising in his place to begin morning service, and wondering to see the congregation so good on such a day, was suddenly startled, as his eye travelled mechanically over to the Hall pew, usually tenanted by Mrs. Darcy in solitary state, to see the characteristic figure of the Squire. His amazement was so great that he almost stumbled in the exhortation, and his feeling was evidently shared by the congregation, which throughout the service showed a restlessness, an excited tendency to peer round corners and pillars, that was not favorable to devotion.

'Has he come to spy out the land?' the Rector thought to himself, and could not help a momentary tremor at the idea of preaching before so formidable an auditor. Then he pulled himself together by a great effort, and fixing his eyes on a shockheaded urchin half way down the church, read the service to him. Catherine meanwhile in her seat on the northern side of the nave, her soul lulled in Sunday peace, knew nothing of Mr. Wendover's appearance.

Robert preached on the first sermon of Jesus, on the first appearance of the young Master in the synagogue at Nazareth:—

'This day is this scripture fulfilled in your ears!'

The sermon dwelt on the Messianic aspect of Christ's mission, on the mystery and poetry of that long national expectation, on the pathos of Jewish disillusion, on the sureness and beauty of Christian insight as faith gradually transferred trait after trait of the Messiah of prophecy to the Christ of Nazareth. At first there was a certain amount of hesitation, a slight wavering hither and thither—a difficult choice of words—and then the soul freed itself from man, and the preacher forgot all but his Master and his people.'

At the door as he came out stood Mr. Wendover and Catherine, slightly flushed and much puzzled for conversation, beside him. The Hall carriage was drawn close up to the door, and Mrs. Darcy, evidently much excited, had her small head out of the window and was showering a number of flighty inquiries and suggestions on her brother, to which he paid no more heed than to the patter of the rain.

When Robert appeared the Squire addressed him ceremoniously,—

'With your leave, Mr. Elsmere, I will walk with you to the rectory.' Then, in another voice, 'Go home, Lætitia, and don't send anything or anybody.'

He made a signal to the coachman, and the carriage started, Mrs. Darcy's protesting head remaining out of window as long as anything could be seen of the group at the church door. The odd little creature had paid one or two hurried and recent visits to Catherine during the quarrel, visits so filled, however, with vague railing against her brother and by a queer incoherent melancholy, that Catherine felt them extremely uncomfortable, and took care not to invite them. Clearly she was mortally afraid of 'Roger,' and yet ashamed of being afraid. Catherine could see that all the poor thing's foolish whims and affectations were trampled on; that she suffered, rebelled, found herself no more able to affect Mr. Wendover than if she had been a fly buzzing round him, and became all the more foolish and whimsical in consequence.

The Squire and the Elsmeres crossed the common to the rectory, followed at a discreet interval by groups of villagers curious to get a look at the Squire. Robert was conscious of a good deal of embarrassment, but did his best to hide it. Catherine felt all through as if the skies had fallen. The Squire alone was at his ease, or as much at his ease as he ever was. He commented on the congregation, even condescended to say something of the singing, and passed over the staring of the choristers with a magnanimity of silence which did him credit.

They reached the rectory door, and it was evidently the Squire's purpose to come in, so Robert invited him in. Catherine threw open her little drawing-room door, and then was seized with shyness as the Squire passed in, and she saw over his shoulder her baby, lying kicking and crowing on the hearthrug, in anticipation of her arrival, the nurse watching it. The Squire in his great cloak stopped, and looked down at the baby as if it had been some curious kind of reptile. The nurse blushed, courtesied, and caught up the gurgling creature in a twinkling.

Robert made a laughing remark on the tyranny and ubiquity of babies. The Squire smiled grimly. He supposed it was necessary that the human race should be carried on. Catherine meanwhile slipped out and ordered another place to be laid at the dinner-table, devoutly hoping that it might not be used.

It was used. The Squire stayed till it was necessary to invite him, then accepted the invitation, and Catherine found herself dispensing boiled mutton to him, while Robert supplied him with some very modest claret, the sort of wine which a man who drinks none thinks it necessary to have in the house, and watched the nervousness of their little parlor-maid with a fellow-feeling which made it difficult for him during the early part of the meal to keep a perfectly straight countenance. After a while, however, both he and Catherine were ready to admit that the Squire was making himself agreeable. He talked of Paris, of a conversation he had had with M. Renan, whose name luckily was quite unknown to Catherine, as to the state of things in the French Chamber.

'A set of chemists and quill-drivers,' he said contemptuously; 'but as Renan remarked to me, there is one thing to be said for a government of that sort, "Ils ne font pas la guerre." And so long as they don't run France into adventures, and a man can keep a roof over his head and a son in his pocket, the men of letters at any rate can rub along. The really interesting thing in France just now is not French politics—Heaven save the mark!—but French scholarship. There never was so little original genius going in Paris, and there never was so much good work being done.'

Robert thought the point of view eminently characteristic.

'Catholicism, I suppose,' he said, 'as a force to be reckoned with, is dwindling more and more?'

'Absolutely dead,' said the Squire emphatically, 'as an intellectual force. They haven't got a writer, scarcely a preacher. Not one decent book has been produced on that side for years.'

'And the Protestants, too,' said Robert, 'have lost all their best men of late,' and he mentioned one or two well-known French Protestant names.

'Oh, as to French Protestantism '—and the Squire's shrug was superb— 'Teutonic Protestantism is in the order of things, so to speak, but *Latin* Protestantism! There is no more sterile hybrid in the world!'.

Then, becoming suddenly aware that he might have said something inconsistent with his company, the Squire stopped abruptly. Robert, catching Catherine's quick compression of the lips, was grateful to him, and the conversation moved on in another direction.

Yes, certainly, all things considered, Mr. Wendover made himself agreeable. He ate his boiled mutton and drank his *ordinaire* like a man, and when the meal was over, and he and Robert had withdrawn into the study, he gave an emphatic word of praise to the coffee which Catherine's house-wifely care sent after them, and accepting a cigar, he sank into the arm-chair by the fire and spread a bony hand to the blaze, as if he had been at home in that particular corner for months. Robert, sitting opposite to him and watching his guest's eyes travel round the room, with its medicine shelves, its rods and nets, and preparations of uncanny beasts, its parish litter, and its teeming bookcases, felt that the Mile End matter was turning out oddly indeed.

'I have packed you a case of books, Mr. Elsmere,' said the Squire, after a puff or two at his cigar. 'How have you got on without that collection of Councils?'

He smiled a little awkwardly. It was one of the books Robert had sent back. Robert flushed. He did not want the Squire to regard him as wholly dependent on Murewell.

'I bought it,' he said, rather shortly. 'I have ruined myself in books lately, and the London Library too supplies me really wonderfully well.'

'Are these your books?' The Squire got up to look at them. 'Hum, not at all bad for a beginning. I have sent you so and so,' and he named one or two costly folios that Robert had long pined for in vain.

The Rector's eyes glistened.

'That was very good of you,' he said simply, 'They will be most welcome.'

'And now, how much *time*,' said the other, settling himself again to his cigar, his thin legs crossed over each other, and his great head sunk into his shoulders, 'how much time do you give to this work?'

'Generally the mornings—not always. A man with twelve hundred souls to look after, you know, Mr. Wendover,' said Elsmere, with a bright, half defiant accent, 'can't make grubbing among the Franks his main business.'

The Squire said nothing, and smoked on. Robert gathered that his companion thought his chances of doing anything worth mentioning very small.

'Oh no,' he said, following out his own, thought with a shake of his curly hair; 'of course I shall never do very much. But if I don't, it won't be for want of knowing what the scholar's ideal is.' And he lifted his hand with a smile toward the Squire's book on 'English Culture,' which stood in the book-case just above him. The Squire, following the gesture, smiled too. It was a faint, slight illumining, but it changed the face agreeably.

Robert began to ask questions about the book, about the pictures contained in it of foreign life and foreign universities. The Squire consented to be drawn out, and presently was talking at his very best.

Racy stories of Mommsen or Von Ranke were followed by a description of an evening of mad carouse with Heine—a talk at Nohant with George Sand—scenes in the Duchesse de Broglie's salon—a contemptuous sketch of Guizot—a caustic sketch of Renan. Robert presently even laid aside his pipe, and stood in his favorite attitude, lounging against the mantel-piece, looking down, absorbed, on his visitor. All that intellectual passion which his struggle at Mile End had for the moment checked in him revived. Nay, after his weeks of exclusive contact with the most hideous forms of bodily ill, this interruption, these great names, this talk of great movements and great causes, had a special savour and relish. All the horizons of the mind expanded, the currents of the blood ran quicker.

Suddenly, however, he sprang up.

'I beg your pardon, Mr. Wendover, it is too bad to interrupt you—I have enjoyed it immensely—but the fact is I have only two minutes to get to Sunday School in!'

Mr. Wendover rose also, and resumed his ordinary manner.

'It is I who should apologize,' he said with stiff politeness 'for having encroached in this way on your busy day, Mr. Elsmere.'

Robert helped him on with his coat, and then suddenly the Squire turned to him.

'You were preaching this morning on one of the Isaiah quotations in St. Matthew. It would interest you, I imagine, to see a recent Jewish book on the subject of the prophecies quoted in the Gospels which reached me yesterday. There is nothing particularly new in it, but it looked to me well done.'

'Thank you,' said Robert, not, however, with any great heartiness, and the Squire moved away. They parted at the gate, Robert running down the hill to the village as fast as his long legs could carry him.

Sunday School—pshaw!' cried the Squire, as He tramped homeward in the opposite direction.

Next morning a huge packing-case arrived from the Hall, and Robert could not forbear a little gloating over the treasures in it before he tore himself away to pay his morning visit to Mile End. There everything was improving; the poor Sharland child indeed had slipped away on the night after the Squire's visit, but the other bad cases in the diphtheria ward were mending fast. John Allwood was gaining strength daily, and poor Mary Sharland was feebly struggling back to a life which seemed hardly worth so much effort to keep. Robert felt, with a welcome sense of slackening strain, that the daily and hourly superintendence which he and Catherine had been giving to the place might lawfully be relaxed, that the nurses on the spot were now more than equal to their task, and after having made his round he raced home again in order to secure an hour with his books before luncheon.

The following day a note arrived, while they were at luncheon in the Squire's angular precise handwriting. It contained a request that, unless otherwise engaged, the Rector would walk with Mr. Wendover that afternoon.

Robert flung it across to Catherine.

'Let me see,' he said, deliberating, 'have I any engagement I must keep?'

There was a sort of jealousy for his work within him contending with this new fascination of the Squire's company. But, honestly, there was nothing in the way, and he went.

That walk was the first of many. The Squire had no sooner convinced himself that young Elsmere's society did in reality provide him with a stimulus and recreation he had been too long without, than in his imperious wilful way he began to possess himself of it as much as possible. He never alluded to the trivial matters which had first separated and then united them. He worked the better, he thought the more clearly, for these talks and walks with Elsmere, and therefore these talks and walks became an object with him. They supplied a long-stifled want, the scholar's want of disciples, of some form of investment for all that heaped-up capital of thought he had been accumulating during a life-time.

As for Robert, he soon felt himself so much under the spell of the Squire's strange and powerful personality that he was forced to make a fight for it, lest this new claim should encroach upon the old one. He would walk when the Squire liked, but three times out of four these walks must be parish rounds, interrupted by descents into cottages and chats in farmhouse parlors. The Squire submitted. The neighborhood began to wonder over the strange spectacle of Mr. Wendover waiting grimly in the winter dusk outside one of his own farmhouses while Elsmere was inside, or patrolling a bit of lane till Elsmere should have inquired after an invalid or beaten up a recruit for his confirmation class, dogged the while by stealthy children, with fingers in their mouths, who ran away in terror directly he turned.

Rumors of this new friendship spread. One day, on the bit of road between the Hall and the Rectory, Lady Helen behind her ponies whirled past the two men, and her arch look at Elsmere said as plain as words, 'Oh, you young wonder! what hook has served you with this leviathan?

On another occasion, close to Churton, a man in a cassock and cloak came toward them. The Squire put up his eye-glass.

'Humph!' he remarked; 'do you know this merryandrew, Elsmere?'

It was Newcome. As they passed, Robert with slightly, heightened color gave him an affectionate nod and smile. Newcome's quick eye ran over the companions, he responded stiffly, and his step grew more rapid. A week or two later Robert noticed with a little prick of remorse that he had seen nothing of Newcome for an age. If Newcome would not come to him, he must go to Mottringham. He planned an expedition, but something happened to prevent it.

And Catherine? Naturally this new and most unexpected relation of Robert's to the man who had begun by insulting him was of considerable importance to the wife. In the first place it broke up to some extent the exquisite *tête-à-tête* of their home life; it encroached often upon time that had always been hers; it filled Robert's mind more and more with matters in which she had no concern. All these things many wives might have resented. Catherine Elsmere resented none of them. It is probable, of course, that she had her natural moments of regret and comparison when love said to itself a little sorely and hungrily, 'It is hard to be even a fraction less to him then I once was?' But if so, these moments never betrayed themselves in word or act. Her tender common sense, her sweet humility, made her recognize at once Robert's need of intellectual comradeship, isolated as he was in this remote rural district. She knew perfectly that a clergyman's life of perpetual giving forth becomes morbid and unhealthy if there is not some corresponding taking in.

If only it had not been Mr. Wendover! She marvelled over the fascination Robert found in his dry cynical talk. She wondered that a Christian pastor could ever forget Mr. Wendover's antecedents; that the man who had nursed those sick children could forgive Mile End. All in all as they were to each other, she felt for the first time that she often understood her husband imperfectly. His mobility, his eagerness, were sometimes now a perplexity, even a pain to her.

It must not be imagined, however, that Robert let himself drift into this intellectual intimacy with one of the most distinguished of anti-Christian thinkers without reflecting on its possible consequences. The memory of that night of misery which "The Idols of the Market Place" had inflicted on him was enough. He was no match in controversy for Mr. Wendover, and he did not mean to attempt it.

One morning the Squire unexpectedly plunged into an account of a German monograph he had just received on the subject of the Johannine authorship of the fourth Gospel. It was almost the first occasion on which he had touched what may strictly be called the *matériel* of orthodoxy in their discussions—at any rate directly. But the book was a striking one, and in the interest of it he had clearly forgotten his ground a little. Suddenly the man who was walking beside him interrupted him.

'I think we ought to understand one another perhaps, Mr. Wendover,' Robert said, speaking under a quick sense of oppression, but with his usual dignity and bright courtesy. 'I know your opinions, of course, from your book; you know what mine, as an honest man, must be, from the position I hold. My conscience does not forbid me to discuss anything, only—I am no match for you on points of scholarship, and I should just like to say once for all, that to me, whatever else is true, the religion of Christ is true. I am a Christian and a Christian minister. Therefore, whenever we come to discuss what may be called Christian evidence, I do it with reserves, which you would not have. I believe in an Incarnation, a Resurrection, a Revelation. If there are literary difficulties, I must want to smooth them away—you may want to make much of them. We come to the matter from different points of view. You will not quarrel with me for wanting to make it clear. It isn't as if we differed slightly. We differ fundamentally—is it not so?'

The Squire was walking beside him with bent shoulders, the lower lip pushed forward, as was usual with him when he was considering a matter with close attention, but did not mean to communicate his thoughts.

After a pause he said, with a faint, inscrutable smile,—

'Your reminder is perfectly just. Naturally we all have our reserves. Neither of us can be expected to stultify his own.'

And the talk went forward again, Robert joining in more buoyantly than ever, perhaps because he had achieved a necessary but disagreeable thing and got done with it.

In reality he had but been doing as the child does when it sets up its sand-barrier against the tide.

CHAPTER XXIII

It, was the beginning of April. The gorse was fast extending its golden empire over the commons. On the sunny slopes of the copses primroses were breaking through the hazel roots and beginning to gleam along the edges of the river. On the grass commons between Murewell and Mile End the birches rose like green clouds against the browns and purples of the still leafless oaks and beeches. The birds were twittering and building. Every day Robert was on the lookout for the swallows, or listening for the first notes of the nightingale amid the bare spring coverts.

But the spring was less perfectly delightful to him than it might have been, for Catherine was away. Mrs. Leyburn, who was to have come south to them in February, was attacked by bronchitis instead at Burwood and forbidden to move, even to a warmer climate. In March, Catherine, feeling restless and anxious about her mother, and thinking it hard that Agnes should have all the nursing and responsibility tore herself from her man and her baby, and went north to Whindale for a fortnight, leaving Robert forlorn.

Now, however, she was in London, whither she had gone for a few days on her way home, to meet Rose and to shop. Robert's opinion was that all women, even St. Elizabeths, have somewhere rooted in them an inordinate partiality for shopping; otherwise why should that operation take four or five mortal days? Surely with a little energy, one might buy up the whole of London in twelve hours! However, Catherine lingered, and as her purchases were made, Robert crossly supposed it must all be Rose's fault. He believed that Rose spent a great deal too much on dress.

Catherine's letters, of course, were full of her sister. Rose, she said, had come back from Berlin handsomer than ever, and playing, she supposed magnificently. At any rate, the letters which followed her in shoals from Berlin flattered her to the skies, and during the three months preceding her return, Joachim himself had taken her as a pupil and given her unusual attention.

'And now, of course,' wrote Catherine, 'she is desperately disappointed that mamma and Agnes cannot join her in town, as she had hoped. She does her best, I know, poor child, to conceal it and to feel as she ought about mamma, but I can see that the idea of an indefinite time at Burwood is intolerable to her. As to Berlin, I think she has enjoyed it, but she talks very scornfully of German *Schwärmerei* and German women, and she tells the oddest stories of her professors. With one or two of them she seems to have been in a state of war from the beginning; but some of them, my dear Robert, I am persuaded were just simply in love with her!

'I don't—no, I never *shall* believe, that independent, exciting student's life is good for a girl. But I never say so to Rose. When she forgets to be irritable and to feel that the world is going against her, she is often very sweet to me, and I can't bear there should be any conflict.'

His next day's letter contained the following:—

'Are you properly amused, sir, at your wife's performances in town? Our three concerts you have heard all about. I still can't get over them. I go about haunted by the *seriousness*, the life and death interest people throw into music. It is astonishing! And outside, as we got into our hansom, such sights and sounds!—such starved, fierce-looking men, such ghastly women!

'But since then Rose has been taking me into society. Yesterday afternoon, after I wrote to you, we went to see Rose's artistic friends—the Piersons—with whom she was staying last summer, and to-day we have even called on Lady Charlotte Wynnstay.

'As to Mrs. Pierson, I never saw such an odd bundle of ribbons and rags and queer embroideries as she looked when we called. However, Rose says that, for "an æsthete"—she despises them now herself—Mrs. Pierson has wonderful taste, and that her wall-papers and her gowns, if I only understood them, are not the least like those of other æsthetic persons, but very *recherché*—which may be. She talked to Rose of nothing but acting, especially of Madame Desforêts. No one, according to her, has anything to do with an actress' private life, or ought to take it into account. But, Robert dear, an actress is a woman, and has a soul!'

'Then, Lady Charlotte:—you would have laughed at our *entrée*.'

'We found she was in town, and went on her "day," as she had asked Rose to do. The room was rather dark—none of these London rooms seem to me to have any light and air in them. The butler got our names wrong and I marched in first, more shy than I ever have been before in my life. Lady Charlotte had two gentlemen with her. She evidently did not know me in the least; she stood staring at me with her eyeglass on, and her cap so crooked I could think of nothing but a wish to put it straight. Then Rose followed, and in a few minutes it seemed to me as though it were Rose who were hostess, talking to the two gentlemen and being kind to Lady Charlotte. I am sure everybody in the room was amused by her self-possession, Lady Charlotte included. The gentlemen stared at her a great deal, and Lady Charlotte paid her one or two compliments on her looks, which *I* thought she would not have ventured to say to anyone in her own circle.'

'We stayed about half an hour. One of the gentlemen was, I believe, a member of the Government, an under-secretary for something, but he and Rose and Lady Charlotte talked again of nothing but musicians and actors. It is strange that politicians should have time to know so much of these things. The other gentleman reminded me of Hotspur's popinjay. I think now I made out that he wrote for the newspapers, but at the moment I should have felt it insulting to accuse him of anything so humdrum as an occupation in life. He discovered somehow that I had an interest in the Church, and he asked me, leaning back in his chair and lisping, whether I really thought "the Church could still totter on a while in the rural districts." He was informed her condition was so "vewy dethperate."

'Then I laughed outright, and found my tongue. Perhaps his next article on the Church will have a few facts in it. I did my best to put some into him. Rose at last looked round at me, astonished. But he did not dislike me, I think. I was not impertinent to him, husband mine. If I might have described just *one* of your days to his high-and-mightiness! There is no need to tell you, I think, whether I did or not.'

'Then when we got up to go, Lady Charlotte asked Rose to stay with her. Rose explained why she couldn't, and Lady Charlotte pitied her dreadfully for having a family, and the under-secretary said that it was one's first duty in life to trample on one's relations, and that he hoped nothing would prevent his hearing her play sometime later in the year. Rose said very decidedly she should be in town for the winter. Lady Charlotte said she would have an evening specially for her, and as I said nothing, we got away at last.'

The letter of the following day recorded a little adventure: —

'I was much startled this morning. I had got Rose to come with me to the National Gallery on our way to her dressmaker. We were standing before Raphael's "Vigil of the Knight," when suddenly I saw Rose, who was looking away toward the door into the long gallery, turn perfectly white. I followed her eyes, and there, in the doorway, disappearing—I am almost certain—was Mr. Langham! One cannot mistake his walk or his profile. Before I could say a word Rose had walked away to another wall of pictures, and when we joined again we did not speak of it. Did he see us, I wonder, and purposely avoid us? Something made me think so.'

'Oh, I wish I could believe she had forgotten him! I am certain she would laugh me to angry scorn if I mentioned him; but there she sits by the fire now, while I am writing, quite drooping and pale, because she thinks I am not noticing. If she did but love me a little more! It must be my fault, I know.'

'Yes, as you say, Burwood may as well be shut up or let. My dear, dear father!'

Robert could imagine the sigh with which Catherine had laid clown her pen. Dear tender soul, with all its old-world fidelities and pieties pure and unimpaired! He raised the signature to his lips.

Next day Catherine came back to him. Robert had no words too opprobrious for the widowed condition from which her return had rescued him. It seemed to Catherine, however, that life had been very full and keen with him since her departure! He lingered with her after supper, vowing that his club boys might make what hay in the study they pleased; he was going to tell her the news, whatever happened.

'I told you of my two dinners at the Hall? The first was just *tête-à-tête* with the Squire; oh, and Mrs. Darcy, of course. I am always forgetting her, poor little thing, which is most ungrateful of me. A pathetic life that, Catherine. She seems to me, in her odd way, perpetually hungering for affections for praise. No doubt, if she got them she wouldn't know what to do with them. She would just touch and leave them as she does everything. Her talk and she are both as light and wandering as thistledown. But still, meanwhile, she hungers, and is never satisfied. There seems to be something peculiarly antipathetic in her to the Squire. I can't make it out. He is sometimes quite brutal to her when she is more inconsequent than usual. I often wonder she goes on living with him.'

Catherine made some indignant comment.

'Yes,' said Robert, musing. 'Yes, it is bad.'

But Catherine thought his tone might have been more unqualified, and marvelled again at the curious lenity of judgment he had always shown of late toward Mr. Wendover. And all his judgments of himself and others were generally so quick, so uncompromising!

'On the second occasion we had Freake and Dashwood,' naming two well-known English antiquarians. 'Very learned, very jealous, and very snuffy; altogether "too genuine," as poor mother used to say of those old chairs we got for the dining-room. But afterward when we were all smoking in the library, the Squire came out of his shell and talked. I never heard him more brilliant!'

He paused a moment, his bright eyes looking far away from her, as though fixed on the scene he was describing.

'Such a mind!' he said at last with a long breath, 'such a memory! Catherine, my book has been making great strides since you left. With Mr. Wendover to go to, all the problems are simplified. One is saved all false starts, all beating about the bush. What a piece of luck it was that put one down beside such a guide, such a living storehouse of knowledge!'

He spoke in a glow of energy and enthusiasm. Catherine sat looking at him wistfully, her gray eyes crossed by many varying shades of memory and feeling.

At last his look met hers, and the animation of it softened at once, grew gentle.

'Do you think I am making knowledge too much of a god just now, Madonna mine?' he said, throwing himself down beside her. 'I have been full of qualms myself. The Squire excites one so, makes one feel as though intellect—accumulation—were the whole of life. But I struggle against it—I do. I go on, for instance, trying to make the Squire do his social duties—behave like "a human."'

Catherine could not help smiling at his tone.

'Well?' she inquired.

He shook his head ruefully.

'The Squire is a tough customer—most men of sixty-seven with strong wills are, I suppose. At any rate, he is like one of the Thurston trout—sees through all my manoeuvres. But one piece of news will astonish you, Catherine!' And he sprang up to deliver it with effect. 'Henslowe is dismissed.'

'Henslowe dismissed!' Catherine sat properly amazed, while Robert told the story.

The dismissal of Henslowe indeed represented the price which Mr. Wendover had been so far willing to pay for Elsmere's society. Some *quid pro quo* there must be—that he was prepared to admit—considering their relative positions as Squire and parson. But, as Robert shrewdly suspected, not one of his wiles so far had imposed on the master of Murewell. He had his own sarcastic smiles over them, and over Elsmere's pastoral *naïveté* in general. The evidences of the young Rector's power and popularity were, however, on the whole, pleasant to Mr. Wendover. If Elsmere had his will with all the rest of the world, Mr. Wendover knew perfectly well who it was that at the present moment had his will with Elsmere. He had found a great piquancy in this shaping of a mind more intellectually eager and pliant than any he had yet come across among younger men; perpetual food too, for his sense of irony, in the intellectual contradictions, wherein Elsmere's developing ideas and information were now, according to the Squire, involving him at every turn.

'His religious foundations are gone already, if he did but know it,' Mr. Wendover grimly remarked to himself one day about this time, 'but he will take so long finding it out that the results are not worth speculating on.'

Cynically assured, therefore, at bottom, of his own power with this ebullient nature, the Squire was quite prepared to make external concessions, or, as we have said, to pay his price. It annoyed him that when Elsmere would press for allotment land, or a new institute, or a better supply of water for the village, it was not open to him merely to give *carte blanche*, and refer his petitioner to Henslowe. Robert's opinion of Henslowe, and Henslowe's now more cautious but still incessant hostility to the Rector, were patent at last even to the Squire. The situation was worrying and wasted time. It must be changed.

So one morning he met Elsmere with a bundle of letters in his hand, calmly informed him that Henslowe had been sent about his business, and that it would be a kindness if Mr. Elsmere would do him the favor of looking through some applications for the vacant post just received.

Elsmere, much taken by surprise, felt at first as it was natural for an over-sensitive, over-scrupulous man to feel. His enemy, had been given into his hand, and instead of victory he could only realize that he had brought a man to ruin.

'He has a wife and children,' he said quickly, looking at the Squire.

'Of course I have pensioned him,' replied the Squire impatiently; 'otherwise I imagine he would be hanging round our necks to the end of the chapter.'

There was something in the careless indifference of the tone which sent a shiver through Elsmere. After all, this man had served the Squire for fifteen years, and it was not Mr. Wendover who had much to complain of.

No one with a conscience could have held out a finger to keep Henslowe in his post. But though Elsmere took the letters and promised to give them his best attention, as soon as he got home he made himself irrationally miserable over the matter. It was not his fault that, from the moment of his arrival in the parish, Henslowe had made him the target of a vulgar and embittered hostility, and so far as he had struck out in return it had been for the protection of persecuted and defenseless creatures. But all the same, he could not get the thought of the man's collapse and humiliation out of his mind. How at his age was he to find other work, and how was he to endure life at Murewell without his comfortable house, his smart gig, his easy command of spirits, and the cringing of the farmers?

Tormented by the sordid misery of the situation almost as though it had been his own, Elsmere ran down impulsively in the evening to the agent's house. Could nothing be done to assure the man that he was not really his enemy, and that anything the parson's influence and the parson's money could do to help him to a more decent life, and work which offered fewer temptations and less power over human beings, should be done?

It need hardly be said that the visit was a complete failure. Henslowe, who was drinking hard, no sooner heard Elsmere's voice in the little hall than he dashed open the door which separated them, and, in a paroxysm of drunken rage, hurled at Elsmere all the venomous stuff he had been garnering up for months against some such occasion. The vilest abuse, the foulest charges—there was nothing that the maddened sot, now fairly unmasked, denied himself. Elsmere, pale and erect, tried to make himself heard. In vain. Henslowe was physically incapable of taking in a word.

At last the agent, beside himself, made a rush, his three untidy children, who had been hanging open-mouthed in the background, set up a howl of terror, and his Scotch wife, more pinched and sour than ever, who had been so far a gloomy spectator of the scene, interposed.

'Have doon wi' ye,' she said sullenly, putting out a long bony arm in front of her husband, 'or I'll just lock oop that brandy where ye'll naw find it if ye pull the house doon. Now, sir,' turning to Elsmere, 'would ye jest be going? Ye mean it weel, I daur say, but ye've doon yer wark, and ye maun leave it.'

And she motioned him out, not without a sombre dignity. Elsmere went home crestfallen. The enthusiast is a good deal too apt to under-estimate the stubbornness of moral fact, and these rebuffs have their stern uses for character.

'They intend to go on living here, I am told,' Elsmere said, as he wound up the story, 'and as Henslowe is still churchwarden, he may do us a world of mischief yet. However, I think that wife will keep him in order. No doubt vengeance would be sweet to her as to him, but she has a shrewd eye, poor soul, to the Squire's remittances. It is a wretched business, and I don't take a man's hate easily, Catherine!—though it may be a folly to say so.'

Catherine was irresponsive. The Old Testament element in her found a lawful satisfaction in Henslowe's fall, and a wicked man's hatred, according to her, mattered only to himself. The Squire's conduct, on the other hand, made her uneasily proud. To her, naturally, it simply meant that he was falling under Robert's spell. So much the better for him, but—

CHAPTER XXIV

That same afternoon Robert started on a walk to a distant farm, where one of his Sunday-school boys lay recovering from rheumatic fever. The rector had his pocket full of articles—a story book in one, a puzzle map in the other—destined for Master Carter's amusement. On the way he was to pick up Mr. Wendover at the park gates. It was a delicious April morning. A soft west wind blew through leaf and grass—

Driving sweet buds, like flocks, to feed in air.

The spring was stirring everywhere, and Robert raced along, feeling in every vein a life, an ebullience akin to that of nature. As he neared the place of meeting it occurred to him that the Squire had been unusually busy lately, unusually silent and absent too on their walks. What *was* he always at work on? Robert had often inquired of him as to the nature of those piles of proof and manuscript with which his table was littered. The Squire had never given any but the most general answer, and had always changed the subject. There was an invincible *personal* reserve about him which, through all his walks and talks with Elsmere, had never as yet broken down. He would talk of other men and other men's' labors by the hour, but not of his own. Elsmere reflected on the fact, mingling with the reflection a certain humorous scorn of his own constant openness and readiness to take counsel with the world.

'However, *his* book isn't a mere excuse, as Langham's is,' Elsmere inwardly remarked. 'Langham, in a certain sense, plays even with learning; Mr. Wendover plays at nothing.'

By the way, he had a letter from Langham in his pocket much more cheerful and human than usual. Let him look through it again.

Not a word, of course, of that National Gallery experience!—a circumstance, however, which threw no light on it either way.

'I find myself a good deal reconciled to life by this migration of Mine,' wrote Langham, 'Now that my enforced duties to them are all done with, my fellow-creatures seem to me much more decent fellows than before. The great stir of London, in which, unless I please, I have no part whatever, attracts me more than I could have thought possible. No one in these noisy streets has any rightful claim upon me. I have cut away at one stroke lectures, and Boards of Studies, and tutors' meetings, and all the rest of the wearisome Oxford make-believe, and the creature left behind feels lighter and nimbler than he has felt for years. I go to concerts and theatres; I look at the people in the streets; I even begin to take an outsider's interest in social questions, in the puny dikes, which well-meaning people are trying to raise all round us against the encroaching, devastating labor-troubles of the future. By dint of running away from life, I may end by cutting a much more passable figure in it than before. Be consoled, my dear Elsmere; reconsider your remonstrances.'

There, under the great cedar by the gate, stood Mr. Wendover. Illumined as he was by the spring sunshine, he struck Elsmere as looking unusually shrunken and old. And yet under the look of physical exhaustion there was a now serenity, almost a peacefulness of expression, which gave the whole man a different aspect.

'Don't take me far,' he said abruptly, as they started. 'I have not got the energy for it. I have been over-working and must go away.'

'I have been sure of it for some time,' said Elsmere warmly. 'You ought to have a long rest. But mayn't I know, Mr. Wendover, before you take it, what this great task is you have been toiling at? Remember, you have never told me a word of it.'

And Elsmere's smile had in it a touch of most friendly reproach. Fatigue had left the scholar relaxed, comparatively defenseless. His sunk and wrinkled eyes lit up with a smile, faint indeed, but of unwonted softness.

'A task indeed,' he said with a sigh, 'the task of a life-time. To-day I finished the second third of it. Probably before the last section is begun some interloping German will have stepped down before me; it is the way of the race! But for the moment there is the satisfaction of having come to an end of some sort—a natural halt, at any rate.'

Elsmere's eyes were still interrogative. 'Oh, well,' said the Squire, hastily, 'it is a book I planned just after I took my Doctor's degree at Berlin. It struck me then as the great want of modern scholarship. It is a History of Evidence, or rather, more strictly, "A History of *Testimony*."'

Robert started. The library flashed into his mind, and Langham's figure in the long gray coat sitting on the stool.

'A great subject,' he said slowly, 'a magnificent subject. How have you conceived it I wonder?'

'Simply from the standpoint of evolution, of development. The philosophical value of the subject is enormous. You must have considered it, of course; every historian must. But few people have any idea in detail of the amount of light which the history of human witness in the world, systematically carried through, throws on the history of the human mind; that is to say, on the history of ideas.'

The Squire paused, his keen scrutinizing look dwelling on the face beside him, as though to judge whether he were understood.

'Oh, true!' cried Elsmere; 'most true. Now I know what vague want it is that has been haunting me for months——'

He stopped short, his look, aglow with all the young thinker's ardor fixed on the Squire.

The Squire received the outburst in silence—a somewhat ambiguous silence.

'But go on,' said Elsmere; 'please go on.'

'Well, you remember,' said the Squire slowly, 'that when Tractarianism began I was for a time one of Newman's victims. Then, when Newman departed, I went over body and bones to the Liberal reaction which followed his going. In the first ardor of what seemed to me a release from slavery I migrated to Berlin, in search of knowledge which there was no getting in England, and there, with the taste of a dozen aimless theological controversies still in my mouth, this idea first took hold of me. It was simply this:—Could one through an exhaustive examination of human records, helped by modern physiological and mental science, get at the conditions, physical and mental, which govern the greater or lesser correspondence between human witness and the fact it reports?'

'A giant's task!' cried Robert; 'hardly conceivable!'

The Squire smiled slightly—the smile of a man who looks back with indulgent, half-melancholy satire on the rash ambitions of his youth.

'Naturally,' he resumed, 'I soon saw I must restrict myself to European testimony, and that only up to the Renaissance. To do that, of course, I had to dig into the East, to learn several Oriental languages—Sanscrit among them. Hebrew I already knew. Then, when I had got my languages, I began to work steadily through the whole mass of existing records, sifting and comparing. It is thirty years since I started. Fifteen years ago I finished the section dealing with classical antiquity—with India, Persia, Egypt, and Judæa. To-day I have put the last strokes to a History of Testimony from the Christian era down to the sixth century—from Livy to Gregory of Tours, from Augustus to Justinian.'

Elsmere turned to him with wonder, with a movement of irrepressible homage. Thirty years of unbroken solitary labor for one end, one cause! In our hurried, fragmentary life, a purpose of this tenacity, this power of realizing itself, strikes the imagination.

'And your two books?'

'Were a mere interlude,' replied the Squire briefly. 'After the completion of the first part of my work, there were certain deposits left in me which it was a relief to get rid of, especially in connection with my renewed impressions of England,' he added dryly.

Elsmere was silent, thinking this then was the explanation of the Squire's minute and exhaustive knowledge of the early Christian centuries, a knowledge into which—apart from certain forbidden topics-he had himself dipped so freely. Suddenly, as he mused, there awoke in the young man a new hunger, a new unmanageable impulse toward frankness of speech. All his nascent intellectual powers were alive and clamorous. For the moment his past reticences and timidities looked to him absurd. The mind rebelled against the barriers it had been rearing against itself. It rushed on to sweep them away, crying out that all this shrinking from free discussion had been at bottom 'a mere treason to faith.'

'Naturally, Mr. Wendover,' he said at last, and his tone had a half-defiant, half-nervous energy, 'you have given your best attention all these years to the Christian problems.'

'Naturally,' said the Squire dryly. Then, as his companion still seemed to wait, keenly expectant, he resumed, with something cynical in the smile which accompanied the words,—

'But I have no wish to infringe our convention.'

'A convention was it?' replied Elsmere flushing. 'I think I only wanted to make my own position clear and prevent misunderstanding. But it is impossible that I should be indifferent to the results of thirty years' such work as you can give to so great a subject.'

The Squire drew himself up a little under his cloak and seemed to consider. His tired eyes, fixed on the spring lane before them, saw in reality only the long retrospects of the past. Then a light broke in them—a light of battle. He turned to the man beside him, and his sharp look swept over him from head to foot. Well, if he would have it, let him have it. He had been contemptuously content so far to let the subject be. But Mr. Wendover, in spite of his philosophy, had never been proof all his life against an anti-clerical instinct worthy almost of a Paris municipal councillor. In spite of his fatigue there woke in him a kind of cruel whimsical pleasure at the notion of speaking, once for all, what he conceived to be the whole bare truth to this clever, attractive dreamer, to the young fellow who thought he could condescend to science from the standpoint of the Christian miracles!

'Results?' he said interrogatively. 'Well, as you will understand, it is tolerably difficult to summarize such a mass at a moment's notice. But I can give you the lines of my last volumes, if it would interest you to hear them.

That walk prolonged itself far beyond Mr. Wendover's original intention. There was something in the situation, in Elsmere's comments, or arguments, or silences which after a while banished the scholar's sense of exhaustion and made him oblivious of the country distances. No man feels another's soul quivering and struggling in his grasp without excitement, let his nerve and his self-restraint be what they may.

As for Elsmere, that hour and a half, little as he realized it at the time, represented the turning-point of life. He listened, he suggested, he put in an acute remark here, an argument there, such as the Squire had often difficulty in meeting. Every now and then the inner protest of an attacked faith would break through in words so full of poignancy, in imagery so dramatic, that the Squire's closely-knit sentences would be for the moment wholly disarranged. On the whole, he proved himself no mean guardian of all that was most sacred to himself and to Catherine, and the Squire's intellectual respect for him rose considerably.

All the same, by the end of their conversation that first period of happy unclouded youth we have been considering was over for poor Elsmere. In obedience to certain inevitable laws and instincts of the mind, he had been for months tempting his fate, inviting catastrophe. None the less did the first sure approaches of that catastrophe fill him with a restless resistance which was in itself anguish.

As to the Squire's talk, it was simply the outporing of one of the richest, most sceptical, and most highly trained of minds on the subject of Christian origins. At no previous period of his life would it have greatly affected Elsmere. But now at every step the ideas, impressions arguments bred in him by his months of historical work and ordinary converse with the Squire rushed in, as they had done once before, to cripple resistance, to check an emerging answer, to justify Mr. Wendover.

We may quote a few fragmentary utterances taken almost at random from the long wrestle of the two men, for the sake of indicating the main lines of a bitter after-struggle.

'Testimony like every other human product has *developed*. Man's power of apprehending and recording what he sees and hears has grown from less to more, from weaker to stronger, like any other of his faculties, just as the reasoning powers of the cave-dweller have developed into the reasoning powers of a Kant. What one wants is the ordered proof of this, and it can be got from history and experience.'

'To plunge into the Christian period without having first cleared the mind as to what is meant in history and literature by "the critical method," which in history may be defined as the "science of what is credible," and in literature as "the science of what is rational," is to invite fiasco. The theologian in such a state sees no obstacle to accepting an arbitrary list of documents with all the strange stuff they may contain, and declaring them to be sound historical material, while he applies to all the strange stuff of a similar kind surrounding them the most rigorous principles of modern science. Or he has to make believe that the reasoning processes exhibited in the speeches of the Acts, in certain passages of St. Paul's Epistles, or in the Old Testament quotations in the Gospels, have a validity for the mind of the nineteenth century, when in truth they are the imperfect, half-childish products of the mind of the first century of quite insignificant or indirect value to the historian of fact, of enormous value to the historian of *testimony* and its varieties.'

'Suppose, for instance, before I begin to deal with the Christian story, and the earliest Christian development, I try to make out beforehand what are the moulds, the channels into which the testimony of the time must run. I look for these moulds, of course, in the dominant ideas, the intellectual preconceptions and preoccupations existing when the period begins.

'In the first place, I shall find present in the age which saw the birth of Christianity, as in so many other ages, a universal preconception in favor of miracle—that is to say, of deviations from the common norm of experience, governing the work of *all* men of *all* schools. Very well, allow for it then. Read the testimony of the period in the light of it. Be prepared for the inevitable differences between it and the testimony of your own day. The witness of the time is not true, nor, in the strict sense, false. It is merely incompetent, half-trained, pre-scientific, but all through perfectly natural. The wonder would have been to have had a life of Christ without miracles. The air teems with them. The East is full of Messiahs. Even a Tacitus is superstitious. Even a Vespasian works miracles. Even a Nero cannot die, but fifty years after his death is still looked for as the inaugurator of a millennium of horror. The Resurrection is partly invented, partly imagined, partly ideally true—in any case wholly intelligible and natural, as a product of the age, when once you have the key of that age.'

'In the next place, look for the preconceptions that have a definite historical origin; those, for instance, flowing from the pre-Christian, apocalyptic literature of the Jews, taking the Maccabean legend of Daniel as the centre of inquiry—those flowing from Alexandrian Judaism and the school of Philo—those flowing from the Palestinian schools of exegesis. Examine your synoptic gospels, your Gospel of St. John, your Apocalypse, in the light of these. You have no other chance of understanding them. But so examined, they fall into place, become explicable and rational; such material as science can make full use of. The doctrine of the Divinity of Christ, Christian eschatology, and Christian views of prophecy will also have found *their* place in a sound historical scheme!'

'It is discreditable now for the man of intelligence to refuse to read his Livy in the light of his Mommsen. My object has been to help in making it discreditable to him to refuse to read his Christian documents in the light of a trained scientific criticism. We shall have made some positive advance in rationality when the man who is perfectly capable of dealing sanely with legend in one connection, and, in another, will insist on confounding it with history proper, cannot do so any longer without losing caste, without falling *ipso facto* out of court with men of education. It is enough for a man of letters if he has helped ever so little in the final staking out of the boundaries between reason and unreason!'

And so on. These are mere ragged gleanings from an ample store. The discussion in reality ranged over the whole field of history, plunged into philosophy, and into the subtlest problems of mind. At the end of it, after he had been conscious for many bitter moments of that same constriction of heart which had overtaken him once before at Mr. Wendover's hands, the religious passion in Elsmere once more rose with sudden stubborn energy against the iron negations pressed upon it.

'I will not fight you any more, Mr. Wendover,' he said, with his moved, flashing look. 'I am perfectly conscious that my own mental experience of the last two years has made it necessary to re-examine some of these intellectual foundations of faith. But as to the faith itself, that is its own witness. It does not depend, after all, upon anything external, but upon the living voice of the Eternal in the soul of man!'

Involuntarily his pace quickened. The whole man was gathered into one great, useless, pitiful defiance, and the outer world was forgotten. The Squire kept up with difficulty awhile, a faint glimmer of sarcasm playing now and then round the straight thin-lipped mouth. Then suddenly he stopped.

'No, let it be. Forget me and my book, Elsmere. Everything can be got out of in this world. By the way, we seem to have reached the ends of the earth. Those are the new Mile End cottages, I believe. With your leave, I'll sit down in one of them, and send to the Hall for the carriage.'

Elsmere's repentant attention was drawn at once to his companion.

'I am a selfish idiot,' he said hotly, 'to have led you into over-walking and over-talking like this.'

The Squire made some short reply and instantly turned the matter off. The momentary softness which had marked his meeting with Elsmere had entirely vanished, leaving only the Mr. Wendover of every day, who was merely made awkward and unapproachable by the slightest touch of personal sympathy. No living being, certainly not his foolish little sister, had any right to take care of the Squire. And as the signs of age became more apparent, this one fact had often worked powerfully on the sympathies of Elsmere's chivalrous youth, though as yet he had been no more capable than any one else of breaking through the Squire's haughty reserve.

As they turned down the newly-worn track to the cottages, whereof the weekly progress had been for some time the delight of Elsmere's heart, they met old Meyrick in his pony-carriage. He stopped his shambling steed at sight of the pair. The bleared, spectacled eyes lit up, the prim mouth broke into a smile which matched the April sun.

'Well Squire; well, Mr. Elsmere, are you going to have a look at those places? Never saw such palaces. I only hope I may end my days in anything so good. Will you give me a lease, Squire?'

Mr. Wendover's deep eyes took a momentary survey, half indulgent, half contemptuous, of the naïve, awkward-looking old creature in the pony-carriage. Then without troubling to find an answer he went his way.

Robert stayed chatting a moment or two, knowing perfectly well what Meyrick's gay garrulity meant. A sharp and bitter sense of the ironies of life swept across him. The Squire humanized, influenced by him—he knew that was the image in Meyrick's mind, he remembered with a quiet scorn its presence in his own. And never, never had he felt his own weakness and the strength of that grim personality so much as at that instant.

That evening Catherine noticed an unusual silence and depression in Robert. She did her best to cheer it away, to get at the cause of it. In vain. At last, with her usual wise tenderness, she left him alone, conscious herself, as she closed the study door behind her, of a momentary dreariness of soul, coming she knew not whence, and only dispersed by the instinctive upward leap of prayer.

Robert was no sooner alone than he put down his pipe and sat brooding over the fire. All the long debate of the afternoon began to fight itself out in the shrinking mind. Suddenly, in his restless pain, a thought occurred to him. He had been much struck in the Squire's conversation by certain allusions to arguments drawn from the Book of Daniel. It was not a subject with which Robert had any great familiarity. Here remembered his Pusey dimly—certain Divinity lectures—an article of Westcott's.

He raised his hand quickly and took down the monograph on 'The Use of the Old Testament in the New,' which the Squire had sent him in the earliest days of their acquaintance. A secret dread and repugnance had held him from it till now. Curiously enough it was not he but Catherine, as we shall see, who had opened it first. Now, however, he got it down and turned to the section on Daniel.

It was a change of conviction on the subject of the date and authorship of this strange product of Jewish patriotism in the second century before Christ that drove M. Renan out of the Church of Rome. 'For the Catholic Church to confess,' he says in his 'Souvenirs,' 'that Daniel is an apocryphal book of the time of the Maccabees, would be to confess that she had made a mistake; if she had made this mistake, she may have made others; she is no longer Divinely inspired.'

The Protestant, who is in truth more bound to the Book of Daniel than M. Renan, has various ways of getting over the difficulties raised against the supposed authorship of the book by modern criticism. Robert found all these ways enumerated in the brilliant and vigorous pages of the book before him.

In the first place, like the orthodox Saint-Sulpicien, the Protestant meets the critic with a flat *non possumus*. 'Your arguments are useless and irrelevant,' he says in effect. 'However plausible may be your objections the Book of Daniel *is* what it professes to be, *because* our Lord quoted it in such a manner as to distinctly recognize its authority. All-True and All-Knowing cannot have made a mistake, nor can He have expressly led His disciples to reward as genuine and Divine, prophecies which were in truth the inventions of an ingenious romancer.'

But the liberal Anglican—the man, that is to say, whose logical sense is inferior to his sense of literary probabilities—proceeds quite differently.

'Your arguments are perfectly just,' he says to the critic; 'the book is a patriotic fraud, of no value except to the historian of literature. But bow do you know that our Lord quoted it as *true* in the strictest sense? In fact He quoted it as literature, as a Greek might have quoted Homer, as an Englishman might quote Shakespeare.'

And many a harassed Churchman takes refuge forthwith in the new explanation. It is very difficult, no doubt, to make the passages in the Gospels agree with it, but at the bottom of his mind there is a saving silent scorn for the old theories of inspiration. He admits to himself that probably Christ was not correctly reported in the matter.

Then appears the critic, having no interests to serve, no *parti pris* to defend, and states the matter calmly, dispassionately, as it appears to him. 'No reasonable man,' says the ablest German exponent of the Book of Daniel, 'can doubt that this most interesting piece of writing belongs to the year 169 or 170 B.C. It was written to stir up the courage and patriotism of the Jews, weighed down by the persecutions of Antiochus Epiphanes. It had enormous vogue. It inaugurated a new Apocalyptic literature. And clearly the youth of Jesus of Nazareth was vitally influenced by it. It entered into his thought, it helped to shape his career.'

But Elsmere did not trouble himself much with the critic, as at any rate he was reported by the author of the book before him. Long before the critical case was reached, he had flung the book heavily from him. The mind accomplished its further task without help from outside. In the stillness of the night there rose up weirdly before him a whole new mental picture—effacing, pushing out, innumerable older images of thought. It was the image of a purely human Christ—purely human, explicable, yet always wonderful Christianity. It broke his heart but the spell of it was like some dream-country wherein we see all the familiar objects of life in new relations and perspectives. He gazed upon it fascinated the wailing underneath checked a while by the strange beauty and order of the emerging spectacle. Only a little while! Then with a groan Elsmere looked up, his eyes worn, his lips white and set.

'I must face it—I must face it through! God help me!'

A slight sound overhead in Catherine's room sent a sudden spasm of feeling through the young face. He threw himself down, hiding from his own foresight of what was to be.

'My, darling, my darling! But she shall know nothing of it—yet.'

CHAPTER XXV

And he did face it through

The next three months were the bitterest months of Elsmere's life. They were marked by anguished mental struggle, by a consciousness of painful separation from the soul nearest to his own, and by a constantly increasing sense of oppression, of closing avenues and narrowing alternatives, which for weeks together seemed to hold the mind in a grip whence there was no escape.

That struggle was not hurried and embittered by the bodily presence of the Squire. Mr. Wendover went off to Italy a few days after the conversation we have described. But though he was not present in the flesh, the great book of his life was in Elsmere's hands, he had formally invited Elsmere's remarks upon it; and the air of Murewell seemed still echoing with his sentences, still astir with his thoughts. That curious instinct of pursuit, that avid, imperious wish to crush an irritating resistance, which his last walk with Elsmere had first awakened in him with any strength, persisted. He wrote to Robert from abroad, and the proud, fastidious scholar had never taken more pains with anything than with those letters.

Robert might have stopped them, have cast the whole matter from him with one resolute effort. In other relations he had will enough and to spare.

Was it an unexpected weakness of fibre that made it impossible?—that had placed him in this way at the Squire's disposal? Half the world would answer yes. Might not the other half plead that in every generation there is a minority of these mobile, impressionable, defenseless natures, who are ultimately at the mercy of experience, at the mercy of thought, at the mercy (shall we say?) of truth; and that, in fact, it is from this minority that all human advance comes?

During these three miserable months it cannot be said—poor Elsmere!— that he attempted any systematic study of Christian evidence. His mind was too much torn, his heart too sore. He pounced feverishly on one test point after another, on the Pentateuch, the Prophets, the relation of the New Testament to the thoughts and beliefs of its time, the Gospel of St. John, the evidence as to the Resurrection, the intellectual and moral conditions surrounding the formation of the Canon. His mind swayed hither and thither, driven from each resting-place in turn by the pressure of some new difficulty. And—let it be said again—all through, the only constant element in the whole dismal process was his trained historical sense. If he had gone through this conflict at Oxford, for instance, he would have come out of it unscathed; for he would simply have remained throughout it ignorant of the true problems at issue. As it was the keen instrument he had sharpened so laboriously on indifferent material, now ploughed its agonizing way, bit by bit, into the most intimate recesses of thought and faith.

Much of the actual struggle he was able to keep from Catherine's view, as he had vowed to himself to keep it. For after the Squire's departure, Mrs. Darcy too went joyously up to London to flutter awhile through the golden alleys of Mayfair; and Elsmere was left once more in undisturbed possession of the Murewell library. There for a while on every day—oh, pitiful relief!— he could hide himself from the eyes he loved.

But, after all, married love allows of nothing but the shallowest concealments. Catherine had already had one or two alarms. Once, in Robert's study, among a tumbled mass of books he had pulled out in search of something missing, and which she was putting in order, she had come across that very book on the Prophecies which at a critical moment had so deeply affected Elsmere. It lay open and Catherine was caught by the heading of a section: 'The Messianic Idea.'

She began to read, mechanically at first and read about a page. That page so shocked a mind accustomed to a purely traditional and mystical interpretation of the Bible that the book dropped abruptly from her hand, and she stood a moment by her husband's table, her fine face pale and frowning.

She noticed, with bitterness, Mr. Wendover's name on the title-page. Was it right for Robert to have such books? Was it wise, was it prudent, for the Christian to measure himself against such antagonism as this? She wrestled painfully with the question. 'Oh, but I can't understand,' she said to herself with an almost agonized energy. 'It is I who am timid, faithless! He *must*—he *must*—know what they say; he must have gone through the dark places if he is to carry others through them.'

So she stilled and trampled on the inward protest. She yearned to speak of it to Robert, but something withheld her. In her passionate wifely trust she could not bear to seem to question the use he made of his time and thought; and a delicate moral scruple warned her she might easily allow her dislike of the Wendover friendship to lead her into exaggeration and injustice.

But the stab of that moment recurred—dealt now by one slight incident—now by another. And after the Squire's departure Catherine suddenly realized that the whole atmosphere of their home-life was changed.

Robert was giving himself to his people with a more scrupulous energy than ever. Never had she seen him so pitiful, so full of heart for every human creature. His sermons, with their constant imaginative dwelling on the earthly life of Jesus, affected her now with a poignancy, a pathos, which were almost unbearable. And his tenderness to her was beyond words. But with that tenderness there was constantly mixed a note of remorse, a painful self-depreciation which she could hardly notice in speech, but which every now and then wrung her heart. And in his parish work he often showed a depression, an irritability, entirely new to her. He who had always the happiest power of forgetting to-morrow all the rubs of to-day, seemed now quite incapable of saving himself and his cheerfulness in the old ways, nay, had developed a capacity for sheer worry she had never seen in him before. And meanwhile all the old gossips of the place spoke their mind freely to Catherine on the subject of the Rector's looks, coupling their remarks with a variety of prescriptions out of which Robert did sometimes manage to get one of his old laughs. His sleeplessness, too, which had always been a constitutional tendency, had become now so constant and wearing that Catherine began to feel a nervous hatred of his book-work, and of those long mornings at the Hall; a passionate wish to put an end to it, and carry him away for a holiday.

But he would not bear of the holiday, and he could hardly bear any talk of himself. And Catherine had been brought up in a school of feeling which bade love be very scrupulous, very delicate, and which recognized in the strongest way the right of every human soul to its own privacy, its own reserves. That something definite troubled him she was certain. What it was he clearly avoided telling her, and she could not hurt him by impatience.

He would tell her soon—when it was right—she cried pitifully to herself. Meantime both suffered, she not knowing why, clinging to each other the while more passionately than ever.

One night, however, coming down in her dressing-gown into the study in search of a *Christian Year* she had left behind her, she found Robert with papers strewn before him, his arms on the table and his head laid down upon them. He looked up as she came in, and the expression of his eyes drew her to him irresistibly.

'Were you asleep, Robert? Do come to bed!'

He sat up, and with a pathetic gesture held out his arm to her. She came on to his knee, putting her white arms round his neck, while he leant his head against her breast.

'Are you tired with all your walking to-day?' she said presently, a pang at her heart.

'I am tired,' he said, 'but not with walking.'

'Does your book worry you? You shouldn't work so hard, Robert—you shouldn't!'

He started.

'Don't talk, of it. Don't let us talk or think at all, only feel!'

And he tightened his arms round her, happy once more for a mordent in this environment of a perfect love. There was silence for a few moments, Catherine feeling more and more disturbed and anxious.

'Think of your mountains,' he said presently, his eyes still pressed against her, 'of High Fell, and the moonlight, and the house where Mary Backhouse died. Oh! Catherine, I see you still, and shall always see you, as I saw you then, my angel of healing and of grace!'

'I too have been thinking of her tonight,' said Catherine softly, 'and of the walk to Shanmoor. This evening in the garden it seemed to me as though there were Westmoreland scents in the air! I was haunted by a vision of bracken, and rocks, and sheep browsing up the fell slopes.'

'Oh for a breath of the wind on High Fell!' cried Robert,—it was so new to her, the dear voice with his accent in it, of yearning depression! 'I want more of the spirit of the mountains, their serenity, their strength. Say me that Duddon sonnet you used to say to me there, as you said it to me that last Sunday before our wedding, when we walked up the Shanmoor road to say good-by to that blessed spot. Oh! how I sit and think of it sometimes, when life seems to be going crookedly, that rock on the fell-side where I found you, and caught you, and snared you, my dove, for ever.'

And Catherine, whose mere voice was as balm to this man of many impulses, repeated to him, softly in the midnight silence, those noble lines in which Wordsworth has expressed, with the reserve and yet the strength of the great poet, the loftiest yearning of the purest hearts—

> *Enough, if something from our hand have power*
>
> *To live and move, and serve the future hour,*
>
> *And if, as towards the silent tomb we go,*

Through love, through hope, and faith's transcendent dower,

   We feel that we are greater than we know.

'He has divined it all,' said Robert, drawing a long breath when she stopped, which seem to relax the fibres of the inner man, 'the fever and the fret of human thought, the sense of littleness, of impotence, of evanescence—and he has soothed it all!'

'Oh, not all, not all!' cried Catherine, her look kindling, and her rare passion breaking through; 'how little in comparison!'

For her thoughts were with him of whom it was said—'*He needed not that anyone should bear witness concerning man, for he knew what was in man.*' But Robert's only response was silence and a kind of quivering sigh.

'Robert!' she cried, pressing her cheek against his temple, 'tell me my dear, dear husband, what it is troubles you. Something does—I am certain—certain!'

'Catherine,—wife—beloved!' he said to her, after another pause, in a tone of strange tension she never forgot; 'generations of men and women have known what it is to be led spiritually into the desert, into that outer wilderness where even the Lord was "tempted." What am I that I should claim to escape it? And you cannot come through it with me, my darling—no not even you! It is loneliness—it is solitariness itself—' and he shuddered. 'But pray for me—pray that *He* may be with me, and that at the end there may be light!'

He pressed her to him convulsively, then gently released her. His solemn eyes, fixed upon her as she stood there beside him, seemed to forbid her to say a word more. She stooped; she laid her lips to his; it was a meeting of soul with soul; then she went softly out, breaking the quiet of the house by a stifled sob as she passed upstairs.

Oh! But at last she thought she understood him. She had not passed her girlhood, side by side with a man of delicate fibre, of melancholy and scrupulous temperament, and within hearing of all the natural interests of a deeply religious mind, religious biography, religious psychology, and—within certain sharply defined limits—religious speculation, without being brought face to face with the black possibilities of 'doubts' and 'difficulties' as barriers in the Christian path. Has not almost every Christian of illustrious excellence been tried and humbled by them? Catherine, looking back upon her own youth, could remember certain crises of religious melancholy, during which she had often dropped off to sleep at night on a pillow wet with tears. They had passed away quickly, and for ever. But she went back to them now, straining her eyes through the darkness of her own past, recalling her father's days of spiritual depression, and the few difficult words she had sometimes heard from him as to those bitter times of religious dryness and hopelessness, by which God chastens from time to time His most faithful and heroic souls. A half-contempt awoke in her for the unclouded serenity and confidence of her own inner life. If her own spiritual experience had gone deeper, she told herself with the strangest self-blame, she would have been able now to understand Robert better—to help him more.

She thought as she lay awake after those painful moments in the study, the fears welling up slowly in the darkness, of many things that had puzzled her in the past. She remembered the book she had seen on his table; her thoughts travelled over his months of intercourse with the Squire; and the memory of Mr. Newcome's attitude toward the man whom he conceived to be his Lord's adversary, as contrasted with Robert's, filled her with a shrinking pain she dare not analyze.

Still all through, her feeling toward her husband was in the main akin to that of the English civilian at home toward English soldiers abroad, suffering and dying that England may be great. *She* had sheltered herself all her life from those deadly forces of unbelief which exist in English society, by a steady refusal to know what, however, any educated university man must perforce know. But such a course of action was impossible for Robert. He had been forced into the open, into the fall tide of the Lord's battle. The chances of that battle are many; and the more courage the more risk of wounds and pain. But the great Captain knows—the great Captain does not forget His own!

For never, never had she smallest doubt as to the issue of this sudden crisis in her husband's consciousness, even when she came nearest to apprehending its nature. As well might she doubt the return of daylight, as dream of any permanent eclipse descending upon the faith which had shown through every detail of Robert's ardent impulsive life, with all its struggles, all its failings, all its beauty, since she had known him first. The dread did not even occur to her. In her agony of pity and reverence she thought of him as passing through a trial, which is specially the believer's trial—the chastening by which God proves the soul He loves. Let her only love and trust in patience.

So that day by day as Robert's depression still continued, Catherine surrounded him with the tenderest and wisest affection. Her quiet common-sense made itself heard, forbidding her to make too much of the change in him, which might after all, she thought, be partly explained by the mere physical results of his long strain of body and mind during the Mile End epidemic. And for the rest she would not argue; she would not inquire. She only prayed that she might so lead the Christian life beside him, that the Lord's tenderness, the Lord's consolation, might shine upon him through her. It had never been her wont to speak to him much about his own influence, his own effect, in the parish. To the austerer Christian, considerations of this kind are forbidden: 'It is not I, but Christ that worketh in me.' But now, whenever she came across any striking trace of his power over the weak or the impure, the sick or the sad, she would in some way make it known to him, offering it to him in her delicate tenderness, as though it were a gift that the Father had laid in her hand for him: a token that the Master was still indeed with His servant, and that all was fundamentally well!

And so much, perhaps, the contact with his wife's faith, the power of her love, wrought in Robert, that during these weeks and months he also never lost his own certainty of emergence from the shadow which had overtaken him. And, indeed, driven on from day to day, as he was by an imperious intellectual thirst, which would be satisfied, the religion of the heart, the imaginative emotional habit of years, that incessant drama which the soul enacts with the Divine Powers to which it feels itself committed, lived and persisted through it all. Feeling was untouched. The heart was still passionately on the side of all its old loves and adorations, still blindly trustful that in the end, by some compromise as yet unseen, they would be restored to it intact.

Some time toward the end of July Robert was coming home from the Hall before lunch, tired and worn, as the morning always left him, and meditating some fresh sheets of the Squire's proofs which had been in his hands that morning. On the road crossing that to the rectory he suddenly saw Reginald Newcome, thinner and whiter than ever, striding along as fast as cassock and cloak would let him, his eyes on the ground, and his wideawake drawn over them. He and Elsmere had scarcely met for months, and Robert had lately made up his mind that Newcome was distinctly less friendly, and wished to show it.

Elsmere had touched his arm before Newcome had perceived any one near him. Then he drew back with a start—

'Elsmere you here! I had an idea you were away for a holiday!'

'Oh, dear, no!' said Robert, smiling. 'I may get away in September, perhaps—not till then.'

'Mr. Wendover at home?' said the other, his eyes turning to the Hall, of which the chimneys were just visible from where they stood.

'No, he is abroad.'

'You and he have made friends, I understand,' said the other abruptly, his eager, look returning to Elsmere; 'I hear of you as always together.'

'We have made friends, and we walk a great deal when the Squire is here,' said Robert, meeting Newcome's harshness of tone with a bright dignity. 'Mr. Wendover has even been doing something for us in the village. You should come and see the new Institute. The roof is on, and we shall open it in August or September. The best building of the kind in the country by far, and Mr. Wendover's gift.'

'I suppose you use the library a great deal?' said Newcome, paying no attention to these remarks, and still eyeing his companion closely.

'A great deal.'

Robert had at that moment under his arm a German treatise on the history of the Logos doctrine, which afterward, looking back on the little scene, he thought it probable Newcome recognized. They turned toward the rectory together, Newcome still asking abrupt questions as to the Squire, the length of time he was to be away, Elsmere's work, parochial and literary, during the past six months, the number of his Sunday congregation, of his communicants, &c. Elsmere bore his catechism with perfect temper, though Newcome's manner had in it a strange and almost judicial imperativeness.

'Elsmere,'—said his questioner presently, after a pause, 'I am going to have a retreat for priests at the Clergy House next month. Father H——,' mentioning a famous High Churchman, 'will conduct it. You would do me a special favor—' and suddenly the face softened, and shone with all its old magnetism on Elsmere—'if you would come. I believe you would find nothing to dislike in it, or in our rule, which is a most simple one.'

Robert smiled, and laid his big hand on the other's arm.

'No, Newcome, no; I am in no mood for H——'

The High Churchman looked at him with a quick and painful anxiety visible in the stern eyes.

'Will you tell me what that means?'

'It means,' said Robert, clasping his hands tightly behind him, his pace slackening a little to meet that of Newcome—'it means that if you will give me your prayers, Newcome, your companionship sometimes, your pity always, I will thank you from the bottom of my heart. But I am in a state just now, when I must fight my battles for myself, and in God's sight only!'

It was the first burst of confidence which had passed his lips to any one but Catherine.

Newcome stood still, a tremor of strong emotion running through the emaciated face.

'You are in trouble, Elsmere; I felt it, I knew it, when I first saw you!'

'Yes, I am in trouble,' said Robert quietly.

'Opinions?'

'Opinions, I suppose—or facts,' said Robert, his arms dropping wearily beside him. 'Have you ever known what it is to be troubled in mind, I wonder, Newcome?'

And he looked at his companion with a sudden pitiful curiosity.

A kind of flash passed over Mr. Newcome's face.

'*Have I ever known?*' he repeated vaguely, and then he drew his thin hand, the hand of the ascetic and the mystic, hastily across his eyes, and was silent—his lips moving, his gaze on the ground, his whole aspect that of a man wrought out of himself by a sudden passion of memory.

Robert watched him with surprise, and was just speaking, when Mr. Newcome looked up, every drawn attenuated feature working painfully.

'Did you never ask yourself, Elsmere,' he said slowly, 'what it was drove me from the bar and journalism to the East End? Do you think I don't know,' and his voice rose, his eyes flamed, 'what black devil it is that is gnawing at your heart now? Why, man, I have been through darker gulfs of hell than you have ever sounded! Many a night I have felt myself *mad—mad of doubt*—a castaway on a shoreless sea; doubting not only God or Christ, but myself, the soul, the very existence of good. I found only one way out of it, and you will find only one way.'

The lithe hand caught Robert's arm impetuously—the voice with its accent of fierce conviction was at his ear.

'Trample on yourself! Pray down the demon, fast, scourge, kill the body, that the soul may live! What are we, miserable worms, that we should defy the Most High, that we should set our wretched faculties against His Omnipotence? Submit—submit—humble yourself, my brother! Fling away the freedom which is your ruin. There is no freedom for man. Either a slave to Christ, or a slave to his own lusts—there is no other choice. Go away; exchange your work here for a time for work in London. You have too much leisure here: Satan has too much opportunity. I foresaw it—I foresaw it when you and I first met. I felt I had a message for you, and here I deliver it. In the Lord's Name, I bid you fly; I bid you yield in time. Better to be the Lord's captive than *the Lord's betrayer!*'

The wasted form was drawn up to its full height, the arm was outstretched, the long cloak fell back from it in long folds—voice and eye were majesty itself. Robert had a tremor of responsive passion. How easy it sounded, how tempting—to cut the knot, to mutilate and starve the rebellious intellect which would assert itself against the soul's purest instincts! Newcome had done it—why not he?

And then, suddenly, as he stood gazing at his companion, the spring sun, and murmur all about them—another face, another life another message, flashed on his inmost sense, the face and life of Henry Grey. Words torn from their context, but full for him of intensest meaning, passed rapidly through his mind: *'God is not wisely trusted when declared unintelligible.' 'Such honor rooted in dishonor stands; such unfaithful makes us falsely true.' 'God is for ever reason: and His communication, His revelation, is reason.'*

He turned away with a slight, sad shake of the head. The spell was broken. Mr. Newcome's arm dropped, and he moved sombrely on beside Robert—the hand, which held a little book of Hours against his cloak, trembling slightly.

At the rectory gate he stopped.

'Good-by—I must go home.'

'You won't come in?—No, no, Newcome; believe me, I am no rash careless egotist, risking wantonly the most precious things in life! But the call is on me, and I must follow it. All life is God's, and all thought—not only a fraction of it. He cannot let me wander very far!'

But the cold fingers he held so warmly dropped from his, and Newcome turned away.

A week afterward, or thereabout, Robert had in some sense followed Newcome's counsel. Admonished perhaps by sheer physical weakness, as much as by anything else, he had for the moment laid down his arms; he had yielded to an invading feebleness of the will, which refused, as it were, to carry on the struggle any longer, at such a life-destroying pitch of intensity. The intellectual oppression of itself brought about wild reaction and recoil, and a passionate appeal to that inward witness of the soul which holds its own long after the reason has practically ceased to struggle.

It came about in this way. One morning he stood reading in the window of the library the last of the Squire's letters. It contained a short but masterly analysis of the mental habits and idiosyncrasies of St. Paul, *à propos* of St. Paul's witness to the Resurrection. Every now and then, as Elsmere turned the pages, the orthodox protest would assert itself, the orthodox arguments make themselves felt as though in mechanical involuntary protest. But their force and vitality were gone. Between the Paul of Anglican theology and the fiery, fallible man of genius—so weak logically, so strong in poetry, in rhetoric, in moral passion, whose portrait has been drawn for us by a free and temperate criticism—the Rector knew, in a sort of dull way, that his choice was made. The one picture carried reason and imagination with it; the other contented neither.

But as he put down the letter something seemed to snap within him. Some chord of physical endurance gave way. For five months he had been living intellectually at a speed no man maintains with impunity, and this letter of the Squire's, with its imperious demands upon the tired irritable bran, was the last straw.

He sank down on the oriel seat, the letter dropping from his hands. Outside, the little garden, now a mass of red and pink roses, the hill and the distant stretches of park were wrapped in a thick, sultry mist, through which a dim, far-off sunlight struggled on to the library floor, and lay in ghostly patches on the polished boards and lower ranges of books.

The simplest religious thoughts began to flow over him—the simplest, childish words of prayer were on his lips. He felt himself delivered, he knew not how or why.

He rose deliberately, laid the Squire's letter among his other papers, and tied them up carefully; then he took up the books which lay piled on the Squire's writing-table: all those volumes of German, French, and English criticism, liberal or apologetic, which he had been accumulating round him day, by day with a feverish toilsome impartiality, and began rapidly and methodically to put them back in their places on the shelves.

'I have done too much thinking, too much reading,' he was saying to himself as he went through his task. 'Now let it be the turn of something else!'

And still as he handled the books, it was as though Catherine's figure glided backward and forward beside him, across the smooth floor, as though her hand were on his arm, her eyes shining into his. Ah—he knew well what it was had made the sharpest sting of this wrestle through which he had been passing! It was not merely religious dread, religious shame; that terror of disloyalty to the Divine Images which have filled the soul's inmost shrine since its first entry into consciousness, such as every good man feels in a like strait. This had been strong indeed; but men are men, and love is love! Ay, it was to the dark certainty of Catherine's misery, that every advance in knowledge and intellectual power had brought him nearer. It was from that certainty, that he now, and for the last time, recoiled. It was too much. It could not be borne.

He walked home, counting up the engagements of the next few weeks—the school-treat, two club field-days, a sermon in the county town, the probable opening of the new Workmen's Institute, and so on. Oh! to be through them all and away, away amid Alpine scents and silences. He stood a moment beside the gray, slowly-moving river, half bidden beneath the rank flower-growth, the tensy and willow-herb, the luxuriant elder and trailing brambles of its August banks—and thought with hungry passion of the clean-swept Alpine pasture, the fir-woods, and the tameless mountain streams. In three weeks or less he and Catherine should be climbing the Jaman or the Dent du Midi. And till then he would want all his time for men and women. Books should hold him no more.

Catherine only put her arms round his neck in silence when he told her. The relief was too great for words. He, too, held her close, saying nothing. But that night, for the first time for weeks, Elsmere's wife slept in peace and woke without dread of the day before her.

www.ingramcontent.com/pod-product-compliance
Lightning Source LLC
Chambersburg PA
CBHW031754150726

47989CB00006B/2717